Trail of Many Stories–A Series

Book One: Sand Beneath

My Feet

Jill Lewis

Prologue

Nascha Begaye sat in her pick-up, stone drunk and close to freezing. The wind howled through the dark night and open windows. It was frigid cold on the high plateau surrounding Many Farms, Arizona. Nascha sat with staring, vacant eyes.

Melody, Nascha's four-month-old daughter, lay tightly strapped in a cradleboard next to Nascha. The baby lay silently wide-awake, the darkness hiding the fear in her brown eyes. Her intense shivering produced just enough heat to keep her alive.

At nearly three in the morning, the cold began a slow sobering, enough to wake Nascha, from her stupor. Although Nascha had only twenty-six years, she felt fifty. Her limbs and joints ached. After a few minutes of shaking and shivering, she brushed the white snow from her straight, black hair. The thought of Melody finally crossed her mind. She slowly looked over at the baby strapped tightly in a traditional Navajo cradle-board. One little bare foot had worked its way out of the binding and blanket.

Nascha stared in complete fascination, seeing only the outline of the little foot. The five toes curled under as if to somehow warm themselves. The gentle sight charmed the young mother.

After several dull minutes, Nascha straightened with a sluggish shiver and reached over and touched the baby's foot. Nascha's body had shielded the baby from most of the snow, but the foot felt stiff and icy.

Fear woke Nascha completely and she gave an ago-nized cry. Moving clumsily, fearfully, she began fumbling with the binding of the cradleboard.

Finally, she freed the baby and pulled her against her chest. The baby felt heavy and cold. Nascha breathed into Melody's mouth, but the baby seemed as stiff as the steering wheel.

With shaking hands, Nascha unzipped the thin jacket she wore. She pulled up her tee shirt and rubbed the baby against her bare breasts. Nascha knew there was no milk and no warmth to be found there, but it was all she could think to do. She pulled her jacket around the baby and rocked back and forth moving her mouth but making no sounds.

For uncounted minutes Nascha rocked silently, trying to share warmth that had abandoned her many hours before. Occasionally she blew alcohol-fumed breath into the baby's stiff lips. The baby did not respond.

Eventually Nascha's milk let down, dripping slowly on the baby, and then running down to Nascha's stomach. The shock of warm milk on her cold belly made Nascha shake violently, and the baby let out a small moan.

Nascha's brain slowly began unthawing. Ignoring the onset of pain that judgment brought–pain much worse than the cold, she quickly put the baby back in the cradleboard and loosely tightened the leather straps. Nascha could not remember how she had ended up on the high plateau or why she had stopped. She turned the key over. The truck made a small growl and went silent.

Melody stirred, and moaned again, this time with more agony. Nascha turned the key over and over. The pick-up only made buzzing sounds.

Anger surged through her innards like a monsoon flash flood through a dry, sandy wash, cold and muddy, the sheer force ripping out large tree trunks and everything in its path.

Nascha pounded the steering wheel, pain shot through her icy hand. A few tears ran down her cheeks. "I would not care if we both die tonight," Nascha's voice hissed.

She looked over at her baby, who was squirming in pain, making little gasping noises. Nascha tried the pick-up again and by some undeserved gesture of grace, the engine roared to life. Nascha looked over at Melody and her laugh was low and bedraggled.

"You are always the lucky one, my baby. I have not known a baby with your big luck."

Henry Yellowhair rubbed his hands together that same cold morning in the pre-dawn. His brown face was handsomely rugged. He quietly left the house and walked to the top of a small hill where he parked his pick-up. He carried a plastic grocery sack of clean socks, underwear and tee shirts. Another plastic sack held a few cans of food and pieces of fruit.

He put the truck in gear, pushed down the clutch and let it roll down the hill then released the clutch. It started.

His Ford was thirteen years old, but because of the meticulous care Henry gave it. The truck ran well, other than the starting problem.

Henry sighed deeply, too tired to start another work-week. He needed to get on the road for the two hour drive to Flagstaff, where he lived and worked construction during the week. The steady job had been a great blessing to him and his wife, Antonia. The decent pay had made it possible to build a small two-bedroom home close to Antonia's parents' traditional Navajo hogan. The hogan was a one-room, eight-sided structure, built out of logs and a mudded roof.

At the beginning of the job, Henry and Antonia had seriously considered moving to Flagstaff to be together during the week. Yet, the thought of moving off the reservation was worse than the gloom when the weekend ended and they faced five days of separation.

Henry felt exhausted, partly because he had watched Antonia nurse their baby late into the night. Antonia had a frail, delicate look, but anyone who knew her would not call her frail. Henry had lay admiring her as she slept. She looked as beautiful as any woman he had ever seen. Baby Lawrence would lazily suck and drift off to sleep. Then with a start he would frantically latch on again, as if his four months had been spent starving, without food. But after a few minutes of fevered activity, sleep would again overtake him and his suck would become unmotivated, his little chin bobbing up and down lazily.

Warm under the heavy quilts, Henry had watched his wife and first born with a feeling of contentment. A kind he had never experienced so intensely in his twenty-four years. His whole being filled up with peace. Henry felt that his past had been made worthwhile and that hope now belonged to them.

Henry understood this sacred moment could not and would not last. He had not worried about getting enough sleep, only savoring the sweetness before him. The joy and goodness soared through him, circled, whirled through Lawrence and Antonia, and back again into him.

The intense early morning cold brought Henry back

quickly. Despite his exhaustion, the lack of cash in his wallet, and the realization of another long, cold workweek, the sweet- ness of the previous night shielded him. His contentment hummed through his lips as he left the Navajo reservation and drove to Flagstaff.

Chapter One

Fourteen years later

When Holland Adams's dad forced her to move from her home in California to Holbrook, Arizona, hate finally had its way and took possession.

Driving away from her home, her friends, her school, away from civilization, Holland's hate cemented, harder than any stone.

Since practically everything of worth became history for Holland, even the preciously few good things left in life seemed eaten alive by hate.

On the drive to Arizona, Holland watched her mother from the back seat of the minivan. For most of her life, Holland lived with anger and resentment because of her mother's depression, but now it all gave way to hate. She hated her mother, who lived in a constant state of shut down.

She also watched her dad, loathing him, feeling annoyed looking at the back of his head, frowning at the small round spot that was starting to bald. She felt hate as he constantly put on, what Holland deemed, a fake smile, and continually looked over to see how her mother was reacting to the trip, reacting to the move. As if someone in a state of shut down would react to anything at all.

Holland had to admit that moving seemed like pretty good shock therapy, but her mother held constant and no reaction came.

Holland glanced over at her little brother, Luke, her one source of good left in the world. But she even felt disgust towards him, because he was always upbeat and positive. Something Holland could not relate with. He looked back at her with nervous blue eyes and messed-up strawberry hair, trying to smile bravely.

The family drove for two days, drove east through northern Arizona, drove across ugly desert, drove for what seemed an eternity. The miles seemed double their length because the mood in the car felt thoroughly hopeless. Only her dad continued to pretend about the prospects.

Several hours into the trip it dawned on Holland that never before would her dad have done something so drastic. Before, he never would have accepted the job offer if it meant a move, never would have thrown the family into chaos like this. Her dad always went to great lengths to hold down the fort with her mother in her state. Her dad seemed energized by the prospects of the move and even though he constantly checked her mother for a reaction he didn't seem concerned enough about no reaction, let alone the havoc the move was causing to the entire family, just another item for Holland to wonder about.

They stopped in Flagstaff, which did not seem too bad because the terrain finally changed. Pine trees wrapped the mountain peaks and, for a moment, Holland felt a small surge of hope.

While Dad filled the car, Holland went inside the convenience store for some water bottles. The man behind the counter asked where they were headed. When she told him Holbrook, he snorted and told her that Holbrook was the armpit of Arizona. Those words completely doused Holland's small glimmer of hope, drowned hope dead.

Back in the car, on the interstate, things got worse. As the family drove towards Winslow, then Holbrook, the land changed from pines, to cedars, to absolutely nothing, just dirt. After a few hours, a sign welcomed them saying, 'Happy Holbrook'. Holland smirked at the word 'happy' paired with Holbrook. An oxymoron if there ever was one, she thought.

It was nearly dark when they pulled off the main road into a cheesy-looking group of cement teepees that called itself the Wigwam Motel. The never-ending dirt became the parking lot.

Her dad smiled brightly, "This will be a fun place to stay for a few weeks until we move into our home."

He looked again nervously at her mother to check for the millionth time her reaction. Nothing.

Holland smiled a small, hard smile, thinking her mother felt as blown away as Holland, with the immense amount of dirt, the immense amount of jack-squat nothing.

The family sat in the car for a few moments in stunned silence. Her dad plastered his fake smile back on, "Well this looks like a fun adventure. Come on Holland let's go see if one of those teepees is available!"

Luke automatically stayed in the car as if to protect their mother. Rolling her eyes, Holland climbed out of the car, secretly curious about what the teepees looked like inside, but knowing she would only feel hate toward whatever she found.

Inside the front office, her dad asked, "Is there an available teepee?"

The man behind the counter looked Native American. He smiled cheerfully and asked, "Where are you folks from and what brings you to Holbrook?"

"We are from California," her dad announced in an artificial way that made Holland cringe, "moving to Holbrook for my new job managing personnel for the mining company."

A renewed surge of hate pulsed through Holland. It felt like having a bucket of cold water dumped on her, except she could feel the water on her insides and the water felt dirty, murky, and foul.

The man behind the counter said, "Glad to meet you. You will love Holbrook. It may not look like much, but the beauty grows on you."

"The beauty?" Holland exclaimed in disgust before she

could stop herself.

"There's more to the area and the people than meets the eye. Will you be going to school here?" The man looked at Holland pleasantly, not seeming to hold her rudeness against her.

A wash of despair and fear joined the hate. The thought of starting a new school in an ugly town, in a school that was mainly Native American, scared Holland, right down to her toes. She smiled a misshapen grimace at the man and walked out the door.

As she walked to the car, Holland saw her mother slumped in the front seat wiping tears from her cheeks. A reaction, Holland thought, her mother was actually having a reaction. The sight did not do much to calm the wave of ugliness and hopelessness that Holland was drowning in.

She climbed in the back seat silently, not wanting to answer the questions in Luke's eyes. Her mother sniffled and tried to cry quietly. Holland sat and tried, but could not find a shred of compassion.

Luke, always kind, always optimistic, could find no words.

Harsh and shrill a barreling train shattered the silence, whistling as if to wake the dead. The track literally ran just yards behind the teepees. The family car vibrated. It felt like a poorly made horror movie. Holland and Luke watched the train thunder past. She looked at her mother, who watched it with a look of sheer terror.

Her dad got back in the car. He looked over at Mother and put his hand on her shoulder, not saying anything, trying to will some hope and optimism into her. It didn't work. Holland knew it didn't work, couldn't work, because her dad possessed no real hope or optimism. How could he, under these circumstances? He turned the car on and pulled slowly over to the teepee in the corner.

Inside, the teepee was surprisingly clean and homey. It smelled like fresh laundry. There were two double beds. Holland walked straight into the bathroom and locked the door. She took a ridiculously long shower, not caring that the family waited to use the bathroom also.

When she finally finished, she stood in front of the mirror and wiped steam from the mirror with her hand. She could see only a jagged image. Her red hair, bright and clear, shone through, no mistaking it.

As Holland stood looking at herself in the mirror she thought, "Unfortunately, it's me standing in a teepee in Holbrook, Arizona, about to start school with a bunch of Native Americans. Unfortunately, I have a Mother in the next room, who is barely hanging on. Unfortunately, I have a Dad who thinks that a fake smile and fake optimism can make things all right. Unfortunately, I have a little brother, who is just as scared as me, but is still genuinely nice. All most unfortunate. More than unfortunate, it is catastrophic."

Still seeing only her bright red hair through the steamy haze, Holland swayed, dizzy and weak, not only from the hot shower, but from the enormity of the situation. It all seemed so irreparable and pointless.

She clutched the sink, head spinning. For some inexplicable reason the spinning reminded Holland of a time long ago, an amusement park ride, a ride with her mother. They sat in a teacup that whirled around. Holland looked at her mother, as she was back then. She saw herself as the little girl laughing.

Holland had forgotten how beautiful her mother was.

Seeing her was a jolt. She seemed another person, not the Mother in bed crying. Her mother's hair was the same color as Luke's, more of a strawberry blond than Holland's fiery red. It was long and thick and fell across her shoulders and into her face. Her eyes radiated green and a few freckles dotted her nose. She was holding onto Holland with one arm and to the teacup with the other, holding on for dear life, and laughing.

Holland watched and felt a lump in her throat as she remembered the young Holland and her mother. The spinning had made her feel light headed and a little sick, but all in a funny way. Finally, the ride came to a stop. The ride smashed Holland into her mother's side. She always had the same nice smell, clean and fresh. The kind of smell she just wanted to bury herself in. They sat for a minute, waiting. Neither said anything. Being close together transcended the ride. It was pure contentment, pure happiness, pure love.

Holland returned to the steamy bathroom and the spinning stopped. She looked at her thin, white arms clutching the sink. She feared she was not strong enough to live her impossible life.

Once more she wiped her hand over the mirror to reveal her face. Her red hair contrasted sharply with her pale skin and clear blue eyes. It startled Holland to see tears running down her cheeks. She wiped those away, trying to wipe away the love she felt for her mother.

With her life unraveling, with all the circumstances that led them to Holbrook, Arizona, and a teepee, and a new, completely crappy life, she felt absolutely no room for love.

But the love hung on her, wrapped in a heavy blanket. A blanket that brought warmth that Holland did not need at the moment and most certainly did not appreciate.

Chapter Two

Melody Begaye sat alone on a huge rock as the evening shadows cast eerie shapes on the high plateau over-looking Chinle, Arizona. The plateau's silence slowly gave way to crickets and the heat of the summer day gave way to the cool of the evening.

During her fourteen years of life, Melody had managed to pick up small scraps of her story. The stories of when her mom, Nascha, in a drunken stupor, nearly let them both freeze to death at this very spot.

Melody had been only four months old when her mother drove to the plateau and fell asleep, on one of the coldest nights of the year. By a stroke of good luck, they survived, with Melody ending up in the hospital with pneumonia.

Because of the plateau incident, the Navajo tribe granted custody of Melody to Nascha's brother Tilden, and his wife Red. They raised her until her mother came back for Melody in the sixth grade.

After several years of heavy drinking, Nascha managed to stay sober for several months and the tribe granted custody back.

Nascha was trying hard to change. Even Melody could see that, watching her faithfully attend AA meetings. Nascha's sincerity at trying to make up for lost time and providing a stable life for Melody was demonstrated with every day's responsible routine.

But the years away from her mom had been hard, even though Uncle Tilden and Auntie Red loved her and tried to help her.

Melody found success at one thing, getting into trouble. She bullied at school and displayed defiance everywhere. Her strong will allowed her to dominate most adults and everyone her own age, everyone except Lawrence Yellowhair.

At the thought of Lawrence, Melody became agitated, frustrated about what? She couldn't quite sort through it.

Melody stood up, unfolded her long legs and started running down the dirt road. She ran faster and faster, running from thoughts of Lawrence. The last time she saw him had been two months ago, at his eighth grade graduation. Of course he was the valedictorian of his class and of course he gave a dumb speech, some weird, little talk about education and the Navajo people, like he was one hundred and fourteen, not merely fourteen.

Melody ran from the memory of sitting in the audience, enjoying the look of surprise on his face when he had noticed her during his lame speech. She ran from the memory of their cutting words to each other afterwards.

"Wow, quite the speech from the Lawrence the Great," she said lightly, even though her heart pounded.

"Probably went right over your head," Lawrence had answered arrogantly.

Melody ran faster still, the sun close to sinking over the horizon, giving the air a golden quality. The world felt still and peaceful, a sharp contrast to how Melody felt.

"I hate Lawrence. I hate Lawrence," she ran, matching the words to the pounding of her feet.

She remembered how later, on graduation night, the school held a dance. Melody went, feeling nervous about the other students, who probably still hated her guts and rightly so. Until two years ago she ruled ruthlessly among her classmates.

She hated to admit it to herself, but the only reason she wanted to attend the stupid dance, was the chance to dance with Lawrence, talk with Lawrence.

Lawrence's family lived on a homestead, which included two small houses, and his grandparent's hogan. His mother was a sister to Auntie Red.

Since she had left, she had only seen Lawrence twice, graduation night and last summer. Lawrence and Melody had walked down to the sandy wash, their childhood playground.

Even though Melody bullied all her classmates, she always got along with Lawrence. As children, playing in the warm sand, they made up towns and stories, keeping them entertained for hours.

Melody quickly discovered that she could not rule over Lawrence, like she easily could most everyone else. He was pleasant and even keeled. She couldn't seem to ruffle him. When she got out of line and used the three cuss words she knew in every sentence, or threw a fit, he ignored her and still enjoyed playing.

He seemed to enjoy her imagination and energy. He was the only one she knew that didn't try to change her in some way. But that had been her childhood, Melody felt sure he would try and change a million things now. Then she wondered if he would even care enough to try.

Melody kept running, her breath coming in gulps, but still she pushed on, faster, thinking about Lawrence, the boy she hated. Would rather think of him than . . . the instantaneous stitch in her side made her bend over, her hands on her knees, gasping for breath.

The thought of her mom stopped her in her tracks, the running over, done. Melody's energy drained. Her mom, who remained sober for a year, had been gone for three days. She left with a friend. Melody knew for sure they were drinking.

She could feel it in every inch of herself. Her worry over her mom trumped any anger and hurt. She prayed her mom would be okay, and tried not think about what could happen, tried but was unsuccessful in having every bad outcome burn in her brain, and then in her gut.

She turned and started walking back in the twilight. Her mom's car now two miles back. She had driven herself to the spot on the plateau, her spot, another drunken binge spot.

Melody shivered, a new wave of worry cascaded over her. For two miles she walked through twilight. Darkness came by the time she reached her mother's old sedan.

She climbed in and felt relief when the old car started. She sat for a minute wondering where she would go. She smiled ruefully thinking how mad her mom would be with her out driving like this. If she got caught she would be in big trouble. But not as much trouble as her mom should be in if she got caught.

Melody drove slowly down the dirt road. She should go home and pray her mom came home safely and that no one found out. Her mom could lose custody again.

Not that it would be that huge, Melody tried to tell herself. She was going to Holbrook in a few weeks to live in the Indian dormitory during the school week. Maybe coming home for the weekends, living again with Auntie Red and Uncle Tilden, and next door to Lawrence, wouldn't be so bad.

But who knew if Tilden and Red would take her again,

after the hell she caused them? Who knew if Lawrence would want her there? He was also going to Holbrook High School, living in the dorms. The thought of him being there made her heart pound against her chest wall a time or two.

She wondered if she drove to Auntie Red's, if Uncle Tilden would tell the tribe. She was tired of living alone. It had been three days and their food was pretty much gone. Her loneliness had driven her to the high plateau, to the spot.

She was a pretty good driver, if she did think so her-self. Driving down the dirt road slowly, she mulled over going to Auntie Red's. What would the outcome be? Her mom would be furious. No, if her mom came back to her senses she would be furious at herself.

At last she made it to the highway. She turned towards Auntie Red's, not home.

Chapter Three

Lawrence Yellowhair felt glad to be left home alone. It rarely happened that all three households of the small homestead were gone at once. His parents, grandparents, and his aunt and uncle's family were all gone to a wedding ceremony. Lawrence didn't mind missing it at all.

Someone needed to stay behind and feed the animals and water the corn. He was the perfect man for the job. In the morning, after everyone left, Lawrence got the feeding and watering done, so that in the heat of the day he could read.

Sitting in the shade he read the entire afternoon, finishing one book and starting on another before late afternoon. After his evening round of chores he shot baskets. The rusted out basketball hoop clanged when the ball hit it, shattering the silence. Lawrence loved basketball and shot until it was too dark to see the hoop.

He showered and made a sandwich and ate it on the porch in the cool of a perfect summer evening.

For the first time that day he felt a little lonesome for everyone. Lawrence brushed that thought away. He didn't leave the porch but sat in the darkness, with just enough moonlight to see a little.

Lawrence jumped up nervously when he saw headlights coming down the dirt road from the highway. He knew everyone would not be home for two more days. His heart raced, as he thought through what he could do if it was unwelcome company.

He stood at the side of the house, in the dark, not to be seen. The person in the car surely could see all the homes were deserted, with not one light on. He wondered if he should slip in the house and get his father's gun.

He could see it was a car and couldn't be sure, but it looked like one occupant. Lawrence decided to wait on the gun. The sedan drove past his home, and his grandparent's hogan, on down to Auntie Red's.

A young woman got out and went and knocked on the front door. Lawrence caught his breath. It looked like Melody. She waited for several moments and knocked again. Lawrence yelled down to her, "No one is home. They're all gone to a wedding."

"Lawrence?"

Lawrence immediately recognized the voice. It was Melody. He walked down the dirt road towards her. His heart pounded in his throat. "Why are you here?"

"Everyone is gone?" Melody sounded downtrodden, something Lawrence never heard from her.

"Yes, to a wedding," he repeated. "Hey why are you driving?" It suddenly dawned on Lawrence.

Melody giggled a little with that question, "I know how to drive. I am a good driver," she said defensively.

Lawrence reached her as she stood on the step of Auntie Red's. Even in the dark he could see her long legs, her hair in a braid. His strong reaction to her being there flustered him. "Why are you driving?" he asked again.

"My, mom . . ." Melody was at a loss for words. Also something Lawrence never witnessed.

"What? What about your mom? Everything okay?"

"Lawrence, if I tell you something, promise me you won't tell, until I decide what to do?" Melody asked urgently.

She always seemed the same, into something, "I don't know if I promise that or not." His annoyance showed through his words.

He was close enough that even in the darkness he could see the anger flare up in her eyes.

"I'm going," she said sounding more sad than angry.

Lawrence grabbed her arm, "First tell me why you are driving and where your mom is."

She stopped short, and put her face close to his, "Okay Lawrence the Great. I'll tell you. She's been gone for three days. I know she's drinking."

Lawrence let go of her arm and stepped back in shock, "How do you know she's drinking? Maybe she's not. You don't know."

"Well Mr. Lawrence, the Idiot. Would my mom leave me alone for three days without telling me anything if she wasn't drinking?"

Lawrence knew she was right, dead on right. He remembered something he overheard Auntie Red telling his mother a few days before, something about Nascha going to a medicine man. He hadn't heard it all, but heard enough to know they questioned the validity of the medicine man. He wondered if he should tell her.

Melody, watching his face, immediately asked, "What? What do you know? Have you heard something?"

"A, A few days ago, I heard Auntie Red telling my mother about your mom going to a medicine man. I could tell they, that they wondered about her choice in one."

"Yeah, so what? I know she's gone to one in Cornfields a few times, for help with staying off the alcohol."

"You do know Melody, that there are upright medicine men and then there are evil ones?" Lawrence questioned.

"Lawrence, don't talk to me like I am some white girl. Of course I know that," Melody's voice showed her disgust.

"Okay, okay. I could just tell they thought he wasn't a reputable one, that's all."

"Well, what's that supposed to mean? And what does it matter? She's drinking!"

Lawrence could not help but to notice how pretty

Melody looked. Every time he saw her it seemed she got prettier. He wished he wasn't so attracted to her.

"How much driving have you done in the past few days?" he asked.

"Today is the first day. I drove up to the plateau."

Lawrence knew the story of her nearly freezing to death, as a baby, on the plateau.

"What made you decide to come here?"

"You know for supposedly being smart you ask really stupid questions."

Lawrence sighed. It was a stupid question. He knew she had nowhere else to go, no other source of help, "I'm sorry. That was a dumb question. What do you want to do now?"

Melody seemed to melt a little, "I don't know I didn't know if I should even come. I'm afraid Tilden will report my mom to the tribe. I don't want her to lose custody, but I'm just, I'm worried about her."

Lawrence thought about Melody living for three days alone, worried, and afraid. He did not blame her for driving away from it all, trying to find help. He felt ashamed of his actions. Since she left in sixth grade, she just brought something out of him. Something he usually did not like. She didn't use to be able to, but since then, she could crawl under his skin so quick.

"Why don't you spend the night at Auntie Red's? In the morning we can figure out what to do," he offered.

The weariness in her voice was evident, "I think I will. Maybe in the morning, we could figure out where to go look for her."

"Okay," Lawrence thought of two of them driving around tomorrow, thought how his parents would react to that, but did not want to argue more with Melody.

"Will you be okay tonight?" Lawrence asked.

"Yeah, of course."

Lawrence looked up at the million stars in the Milky Way. He loved summer nights. He shocked himself by saying, "Should we walk down to the wash?"

"Okay," he could hear the surprise in Melody's voice.

Even in the dark, both could find their way easily to the path that led down into the deep, sandy wash.

They walked to a huge, old cottonwood log, long ago washed down in a flash flood during the monsoons.

They sat in silence on the log, which still held warmth from the day. Lawrence had to admit as easily as Melody could get under his skin, she was the only one he could sit on a log with, in the dark, and feel comfortable. So much about them together he could not explain.

After a while he asked, "Why do you think she went back to drinking?"

After a longer while she sighed, "I don't know. She's been doing so good. We follow all this AA crap, and actually, it felt like it helped."

"Do you think it could have anything to do with the bad medicine man?" Lawrence asked, feeling a chill down his back, breaking through the warmth of the evening.

Melody must have felt the chill too, because she shivered slightly before answering, "I have no idea. But it's probably all I have to go on right now. I know she went to him three times. She heard he could help her with cravings for alcohol."

Lawrence reached over and took her hand, "I'm sorry Melody. You shouldn't have to go through any of this."

"Yeah, no one in the world should have to go through anything," she said with sarcasm in her voice.

"I'm serious Melody. I wish you didn't have to experi-ence this."

"Well I am experiencing it. I'm smack dab in the middle of it. What do I do about that?"

Lawrence reached over and pulled her face towards him. He kissed her softly and then again with almost a ferocity. He pulled away, feeling shocked at his actions. The look on her face let him know she was shocked also.

"Our first kiss," she said quietly.

"No, our first kiss was in this wash when your mom came to take you and you came down here to tell me goodbye, then you kissed me," Lawrence softly corrected her.

"I remember. I beat up the principal's son. Auntie Red came to pick me up at school and as soon as we got home I ran down here. She let me stay and I spent the night here, in the wash. The next morning, my mom came. I couldn't believe it."

"I missed you, and I was relieved to see you go," he replied honestly.

"Really?"

"Really," he answered.

Melody put her arms around his neck and kissed him. His head felt light, and his toes tingled, which caused him to laugh.

"Did I do it wrong?" she asked embarrassed.

"No, I'm sure you didn't do it wrong," he said convincingly.

"Why, why did you laugh?"

"Because this is crazy," he replied.

With that he got up and ran through the darkness out of the wash.

Chapter Four

When Holland finally left the bathroom, her mother was lying on one of the double beds, facing the wall. Her eyes were closed but Holland figured she was awake. Her dad and Luke sat on the other bed, propped on pillows, watching TV. Luke stuck his tongue out at her and smiled. Her dad flashed his fake, optimistic grin, to hide his annoyance at Holland being in the bathroom for over an hour.

Holland could have cared less. She scowled until Dad got up and moved over to her mother's bed. Holland crawled in next to Luke, with her back to him, facing the other wall of the teepee.

The blare of another train passed by and shook the tepee. A fine state of affairs, Holland thought. She was about to start high school, living in a teepee, and trying not to interact with her completely pathetic family. And the biggest crud of all, she was acting exactly like her mother.

Tears burned, trying to escape Holland's eyes. Luke, saying nothing, scooted close and rubbed her arm. Luke, living the same miserable life, still remained thoughtful and sweetly funny. Luke, small for a ten year old, had to be as scared as she felt.

Holland wiped her tears away and rolled over to face him and whispered, "Let's go check out this stupid town tomorrow, and find more things to hate about it."

Luke laughed quietly and nodded.

The next morning, when Holland woke up, her dad had left to check out the new job site. Her mother again faced the wall. Luke sat, cross-legged, playing a game on his iPod. Holland got up and dug some shorts and a T-shirt out of her suitcase, went in the bathroom to dress and pull her hair into a pony tail.

Quietly they left the teepee. A grocery store stood across the street. They walked over and bought donuts and chocolate milk. Walking a couple more blocks they found the high school. Past the worn-out campus they walked then up to the football field. The field was cut into the side of the hill. Sandstone boulders extended up from the field, lining three sides, like a natural amphitheater.

Luke asked if they could go find his school. Walking down from the field Holland saw some buildings with Native American geometric designs on the sides. Tiisyatin Residential Hall, a sign announced. The buildings looked deserted, making her feel even more empty, totally validating her hatred for it all.

A few blocks east they found Luke's school, Hulet Middle School. They walked around another deserted campus.

"Hate to tell you this, Luke. I didn't think it was possible. But your school looks even more desolate than mine," Holland's words sounded as dry as her mouth.

Luke smiled, "It doesn't look that bad, at least grass is growing around the school."

The day quickly grew hot but they kept walking. Several blocks down they hit another main road. There stood a little convenience store and gas station. Next to them, a peculiar gift shop, sat right next to the train tracks.

They walked into the convenience store and bought a soda. Nothing like sugar and then more sugar to drown sorrows, Holland thought. They saw a flyer taped on the glass door about a town swimming pool.

Luke asked the clerk where it was and she told them it was several blocks north. Luke looked at Holland and she knew exactly what he was thinking.

"We don't have our swim suits. Let's save swimming for another day."

They walked next door to the gift shop. Holland walked in, leaving Luke staring up at the twenty foot cement Tyrannosaurus Rex that looked more stupid than scary. The outlandish dinosaur stood guarding the shop's entry. Holland walked with disgust past it.

Inside the store, the heavy smell of incense filled her nostrils. Bins of rocks and shelves of cheap Native-American-looking stuff lined the isles. For a few minutes Holland browsed, looking at dusty curios.

A horrific screeching knocked Holland to her knees. It was not the train sound Holland had heard several times since they arrived. A grinding crash, accompanied by the blaring train whistle vibrated the ground. The scraping of metal went on and on as the train dragged something down the track.

The noise and rumbling were so intense Holland felt sure the train would come through the wall and run her over. She scrambled to her feet, knocking over a display, and ran outside to find Luke pressing against the obnoxious dinosaur, pale and horrified. Holland turned and saw, what was a pick-up, torn in half, completely mashed.

The entire front of the truck was gone, leaving only the back end. The train must have hit it, torn it in half and took the front with it, pushing it up the tracks. In a blinding flash the back end of the pick-up caught fire.

The train, still rattling by, screeched and blared so loudly that Luke could not hear her shouting. He stood, not blinking, not moving. Holland ran to him and grabbed him, but he would not move his feet. He felt as heavy as stone.

Holland grabbed Luke's face and turned it. His eyes finally focused on her, but registered no emotion. His face felt cold and clammy between her hands. Holland heard more screeches and the train started to slow, but the sound only in-tensified. The ground continued to vibrate.

Luke looked back at the train and the pick-up, causing his face to scrunch strangely as Holland held it firmly between her two hands. The air grew dark with dust, and heavy with noise. Holland could feel the heat of the burning pick-up. She tugged on Luke's face to force him to look back at her.

And then, just as abruptly as it started, all went quiet. The train somehow finally came to a stop. The smell of gasoline intensified. The quiet roared as loud as the noise.

Luke turned his eyes back to Holland. He finally blinked and a few tears ran down his face, making dusty streaks.

Holland pulled Luke to sit down in the shadow of the dinosaur and wrapped her arms around him. Sirens pierced the quiet. The grime hung in the air, not finding its way back to the ground. Gasoline smell burned their noses.

They sat in the quiet, dirty air, for a long while, not thinking clearly enough to come up with a plan. Finally, a police officer came and stood over them, "Did either of you see what happened?"

With a new wave of shock Holland looked over at Luke, shook her head no, and the officer looked at Luke. Luke slowly nodded yes.

The officer kneeled beside them, "What did you see son?"

Luke again blinked a few times, "That driver must not have seen the train . . . well he must have known . . . the bars came down to stop traffic, but the man drove around them."

The realization of what Luke witnessed settled in with more force on Holland. The officer asked a few more questions and patted Luke on the shoulder, telling him not to leave.

For a long time Holland and Luke sat against the dinosaur, watching the burning pickup. A fire truck sprayed water, but the flames fought on. The burning smoke made it hard to breathe but neither tried to move.

Across the street Holland noticed a Native American man. He was tall and thin and had a long braid. He stood with a bizarre smile on his face. It chilled Holland to see his reaction to the tragedy. She wanted to point him out to Luke, but the man honestly scared her, so she kept quiet, wondering if Luke noticed.

Then their dad showed. Holland wondered what time it was, how her dad knew, but did not ask. Her dad sat down next to them and leaned against the dinosaur. He sat for several moments with his hand on Luke's leg, "Are you ready to go home, Luke?"

The thought of her dad asking that question, infuriated Holland to the core. The hate sloshed up and spilled out.

"Home? What home? A teepee?" Holland yelled in disgust.

Luke looked at Holland wearily, which fueled her anger. "Dad this is crazy! Why are we here? This place must be hell! Look what Luke has been through. Let's go back to Sacramento!" She glared at her dad until he put his head down.

Then Holland was spent. She leaned back against the dinosaur. Luke locked his arm through hers, which did not surprise her. But what he said shocked her, to the core.

"Holland, please stop. It was terrible. But I am sick of you acting like I can't handle things, like I can't figure anything out. You act like I am Mother. I'm not. I'm sick of it."

Holland wanted to tell him that she hadn't thought that, but wondered if she did. She wanted to say that what she really worried about was if she could handle it. But she could say nothing.

Her dad wiped tears away from his eyes, but did not put on the fake smile and act optimistic. He got up and took Luke's hand and pulled him up. Then offered his hand to Holland, but she ignored him and stood up on her own.

When they finally made it back to the teepee, Holland did not hog the bathroom like she had the previous night. They all took quick showers. Her dad went and bought hamburgers for supper, but when he got back, the fries were cold and Holland couldn't swallow. She wanted some real food, and to eat it in a real house, in a real town not hell.

Nobody told Mother what happened. She had to have heard all the noise. Holland wondered if her mother jumped up when she heard the train wreck, or if she had just lain in the bed waiting to be run over.

Nobody discussed any of it. Finally, a few hours later, when they were all in bed, Luke quietly said, "Mom." Holland would have bet good money that her mother was awake but no answer came.

Chapter Five

The next morning Melody woke up later than she wanted to. She slept soundly on top of the covers on her cousin, Sage's, bed. She hurried and showered and put the same clothes back on.

Melody walked to Lawrence's home. She found him coming in from his chores. He smiled, acting a little embarrassed, "Do you want some breakfast?"

"I'm starving."

"I'll cook some scrambled eggs," Lawrence offered.

Melody sat and watched him cook breakfast. When he sat a plate of food in front of her, she smiled, "You do better on your own that I do. I just lived on cereal."

"For three days?" Lawrence acted surprised.

"Basically yes, and some good peaches from Canyon

De Chelly."

Lawrence watched her as she quickly ate.

When she finished, Melody said, "Let's drive to Corn-fields."

Lawrence flinched, "I don't know Melody. Neither of us has a license."

"No one will ever know. And if you don't go with me I'm going alone. I'm going to talk to the medicine man and try and find my mom."

"Did you try calling her?" Lawrence asked.

"Yeah, this morning, and basically constantly the last three days," Melody looked at him like he was stupid. "Look I don't blame you if you won't go, but I have to."

"Okay." Lawrence answered.

"Okay, what?"

"Okay, I'll go with you. I have to be home by this evening to do the chores," Lawrence replied hesitantly.

Melody grinned. "Lawrence Yellowhair, you try to act all traditional and upright, but underneath it all, you are a rebel just like me."

"Don't," Lawrence answered angrily, "you ruin things

when you talk too much."

Melody flushed, feeling just as angry.

They washed the dishes and walked down to the car, "Do you want to drive?" Melody asked, taunting.

Lawrence looked at her, nodding his head in disgust. "Yeah!" he said, surprising her. "I'm a better driver than you, no question."

He got in and turned the radio up loud. They drove to Cornfields on a beautiful summer morning. Melody almost forgot the urgency of their errand.

With Melody giving directions, they turned off the highway, on the dirt road to the medicine man's hogan. They drove over the cattle guard and slowly approached the hogan. Melody looked at Lawrence. He looked as nervous as she felt.

They both got out of the car and walked timidly to the door. The sun was now hot in the sky, but the air felt cold and unwelcoming. Lawrence knocked hard, no answer. He turned to Melody and shrugged his shoulders in relief.

"Knock again," she whispered.

Lawrence knocked again. There was no way anyone in the one-room hogan would not hear it. Melody tried the door. It was locked. They walked around to the small window and peered in. There was a wood stove in the middle of the room and a small kitchen setup on one side. Another side had a small cot. It looked like most any hogan.

"I don't know what to do," Desperation came through Melody's voice.

"Maybe it means he is not with your mom," Lawrence said.

"Maybe it means he is," Melody answered.

They got back in the car. Melody sighed. "We are closer to my house than yours. Let's go look. Maybe she came home."

They drove in silence for the forty five minute drive to Melody's. At last they pulled up to the small home. Melody pulled out her key to unlock the door. Before she got the door unlocked, it opened. Nascha stood with red eyes and a haggard face.

"Mom!"

"Oh, Melody," was all Nascha could say before she began crying. Her mom looked at Lawrence and cried harder.

The three stood in embarrassment. After several moments of awkwardness, in which Melody could think of not one thing to say, Lawrence finally spoke.

"Maybe I should go," then as if realizing he had no way to go, he looked at Melody.

"I'm driving Lawrence home," Melody stated.

Nascha looked more miserable with that information but could not answer and walked back in the house.

Melody stood looking at Lawrence, holding back tears. She knew she looked pitiful and it felt like the last straw.

Lawrence put his hand on her shoulder, not saying anything, he hugged her.

"I don't want your pity."

Lawrence pulled back, "I don't pity you Melody. That's one thing I could never feel for you."

"Good. Let's go. Let me drive," she said trying not to sound like she was crying.

It was a long, quiet drive. As they turned off the highway towards Lawrence's home, he asked, "Are you excited to go live in the dorm in Holbrook?"

Melody glanced at him and shrugged her shoulders, "Yeah, whatever, it will be fun." Then she turned and really looked at him. "Wait a minute," she said, life coming back into her. "You have never lived away from home before, have you? Oh dear, Lawrence the Great will be homesick!"

Lawrence smiled, like he was willing to be ridiculed, if it cheered her up. "I'll just have to cry myself to sleep at night," he answered.

"Lawrence, I'm scared to leave my mom alone," Melody became serious again.

"I don't blame you."

"What if she falls apart? What if this is the beginning of a lot of terrible things?" Melody was fighting back tears again.

"What if this is an isolated incident and she does really well," Lawrence said, sounding one hundred and fourteen. "I wish we knew, Melody."

They pulled up to Lawrence's house.

"Don't tell Auntie Red and Uncle Tilden," Melody warned.

"Don't worry. It's best if my folks don't know about it all, especially the driving. But they might figure out someone stayed in their home," Lawrence smiled.

"They will never know, trust me," Melody answered

assuredly

    "Well, I'll see you in a few weeks. We'll take over the dorm," he said, trying to sound brave.

    Lawrence got out. Melody watched him walk into the house and she drove the car slowly down the dirt road.

Chapter Six

That night Luke woke up screaming, yelling, pleading with the man not to drive through the train guard.

Holland sat up in bed, hugged him and talked quietly until he woke up enough to realize it was a dream. She could feel his heart pounding, and he was in a cold sweat. When he finally fell back asleep, Holland lay awake for a long time. Her dad, sitting on the edge of his bed, climbed back in and her mother stifled a sob.

Luckily, the next few days went surprisingly fast. Every morning when Holland woke, her dad had left for work in the company truck, and her mother lay facing the wall. Her mother's mood did not lighten, but seemed to grow heavier every day, so heavy it felt tangible. Holland sometimes wondered if her mother understood about the train wreck and that Luke witnessed it. Holland didn't know if the train wreck in the teepee could be any worse.

Every morning, Luke would be awake sitting on the bed cross-legged playing some game. Since the train wreck, Luke was quieter and even nicer, all of which scared the heck out of Holland. He was too polite to even turn the TV on while they slept.

Holland and Luke would dress, quietly leave the teepee, buy donuts and milk, and then explore the town. Holbrook wasn't big, except when walking it. Every day they would walk by their soon-to-be home. The house painters didn't seem in too big of a hurry to finish their work.

They walked the town, every street several times, streets named Navajo Blvd, Hopi Drive, and the most ironic of all, Bucket of Blood Street, which ran parallel to the train tracks.

Walking one day, Holland tried to talk to Luke, "I know you are handling it, Luke," she said remembering the conversation they had under the dinosaur. "I also know you have nightmares every night."

Luke was quiet for several steps, "Sorry I wake everyone up with them."

"It's not your fault. None of this is your fault!" Holland answered in a flame.

"Whose fault is any of this?" Luke asked simply.

Holland didn't have an answer for that. She felt anger towards the man that committed suicide, even though he was dead, and anger that he had been crazy enough to do some- thing so drastic in front of her brother. Holland realized the man could not have known he did it in front of her brother, but she still felt anger.

Holland wondered if the man planned it or if it came as a spur of the moment decision. She wondered a million things about the man. It made her wonder things about her mother and she hated that all the more. Holland did not share those thoughts with Luke, the thoughts that somehow the man's death and her mother seemed connected.

Holland wanted to comfort Luke, but soon realized it was nearly impossible for someone filled with hate and anger to offer any comfort. Each time, in the end, Luke gave the com- fort.

Holland could not stop wondering about the Native

American man with the frightening smile at the wreck. She could not think about him without feeling fear, then anger. She grew sick of thinking, of wondering, of the never ending hate and anger towards her life and now Holbrook.

A few times she heard Dad trying to speak with Luke about it. That, of course, was one more thing to anger Holland. She judged her dad, if he could comfort, possessed one ounce of ability to comfort, why the hell did he not comfort his wife?

Wandering Holbrook, they found a Dairy Queen, every convenience store, and an old county courthouse that had been turned into a museum. Holland actually enjoyed that place. The museum had a bookstore, so they each bought a book. Luke's was about Navajos. Holland's told about the history of the area. Holbrook was a town straight from the Wild West.

Somehow mornings felt normal, safer, and the most hopeful. When Holland woke the next few mornings, Luke was reading his book. He would fill Holland in with facts about Navajos, "Did you know we are right next to the Navajo reservation?"

Holland laughed loud. She hoped she woke up her

mother. Luke put his finger to his mouth to quiet her, looking over at their mother, concerned. Holland did not care. Most nights Luke woke in a nightmare and cold sweat. She felt relieved to see him acting happy and normal in the morning.

Holland continued to speak loudly, "School starts tomorrow, and we haven't found that swimming pool."

Holland dug out some clothes and her swimsuit from her suitcase and went into the bathroom to dress.

While Holland was dressing, remembering Luke's bad night, the never-ending, totally-unpredictable hate flooded through her. Impulsively, she opened the bathroom door. "Mother!" she yelled loudly. Her mother and Luke both jumped a mile.

Luke looked horrified. Her mother rolled over, with eyes swollen and red, like she had been crying since she got into that teepee bed. Neither could say a thing. They just looked at each other for a few minutes.

Then her mother started sobbing, "Holland, sweetie, I am sorry, I am so sorry." In an instant Luke was at her side. Her mother looked at him and started again, "I am sorry." Luke looked like he was fighting back tears and glared at Holland.

Watching the complete weirdness of the spectacle for a few minutes, Holland tried to come up with a word to describe it. Her mind fumbled. Holland loved words and they usually came easily to her. She could always pull one out that perfectly described a situation. Her mind churned and churned, adding to her frustration.

Finally, Holland stormed out of the teepee, slamming the door. She stood waiting for Luke. Just when she felt her anger peaking and considered leaving him, he came out quietly.

Luke looked at Holland with sadness, and frustration. His look was all the punishment Holland needed for her behavior. With burning eyes, Holland tromped to the grocery store, Luke following. In the store they bought the usual donuts and milk, trying to ignore each other as much as possible.

"Pitiful," she yelled, once back outside the store.

"What?" Luke asked annoyed.

"I finally figured out the word. Pitiful."

"You're pitiful," Luke replied.

They sat on their breakfast bench and ate their donuts giving each other the silent treatment. As the heat set in, they started the long walk to the pool.

Walking that far without speaking gave Holland too much time to think. It took several blocks for remorse to set in. Pitiful was the perfect word to describe her. She was a pitiful girl, in a pitiful town, living in a pitiful teepee, with a pitiful mother who did not seem to have the desire, or the will, or the ability to just live.

The Native man at the train wreck appeared in her mind. This time he looked right at her and smiled his terrible smile. Holland felt a cold chill in the heat of the sun. Her life now officially felt like a twilight zone.

Holland was almost four when Luke was born. She could remember her mother being different. She wondered if Luke could remember when things were different. She wanted to ask him, to talk to him about it, but her pride kept her silent.

Holland remembered when life was a far cry from pitiful. She remembered when her mother got up every morning, and dressed and made breakfast. She had memories of her mother laughing, teasing her dad, or helping her do things, of her taking care of Luke. She could remember when her parents looked like love.

Holland tried to remember exactly when the depression began, but could not. She wondered when it took hold, its ugly claws and tentacles, pulling her mother out of her body, leaving only the shell.

A block before the pool, Luke stopped and turned to Holland, "I'm not mad anymore. Are you?"

Holland smiled and felt ashamed. Her little brother, small, strawberry hair, blue eyes, was always a bigger person than she would ever be.

At last they arrived at the pool, hot and sweaty under the August sun. Up close the pool looked old and run down, Holland felt self-conscious of her skinny, white body in a swim-suit. She glanced around, wondering if there would be anyone to talk to; she could see no one and quickly jumped in the pool. The pool was clean and the water felt wonderful.

Luke started talking to a young Native boy. Holland swam for a while and then sat in the warm sun on her towel. She thought of California, of being in a beautiful and much newer pool there, surrounded by friends. She could see no one here she would even want to interact with.

When she could feel the heat burning her fair skin, she

jumped back in the pool. As she dog paddled around the pool, a little boy running along the side yelled to his mother, "Hey look at that hair. It's so red!" The little boy's mom didn't shush him; she only stared at Holland as if in agreement.

Holland thought the boy talked funny, had some kind of accent which kind of chipped his words or something. She couldn't really put her finger on it. Suddenly something as simple as the way the young boy talked, and what he said, became a funnel for a new load of anger to bubble up and pour out. That was how the anger, and hate operated, never, ever content.

Holland motioned for Luke to come. They were leaving. She could see the disappointment on his face. He was talking and laughing with a few kids, looking happy. Luke rolled his eyes, but did not argue or complain. He just came.

They started sloshing home in wet flip-flops and dripping swim suits under their T-shirts. After a few blocks Luke asked, "Why did we have to leave"?

"A little boy talked about my hair," Holland felt ashamed of her words, of herself. "You know what, shut up Luke."

Luke complied and for several more blocks they

walked in silence, the water quickly evaporated and the heat set in.

One block later, Holland started talking to herself. Something she did when she became over-the-top stressed. "You stupid, stupid, selfish girl," she said, oblivious of what she was doing.

With each tedious step, Holland felt more demoralized, more ashamed, more angry, more completely a complete creep of a person. Until finally the excruciating weight of her pathetic-ness rested right on top of her head, and she could not walk another step.

She sat down on the curb and began sobbing. An ocean of tears stored in her skinny, white body flooded out of her as she sat sobbing right on Main Street. The curb that many cars were driving past. The curb that at any other time she would have shuddered in humiliation at the thought of do-ing what she was doing.

Holland's sadness rolled up and out of her, in never ending waves. Her crying became so intense, that she strug-gled to catch her breath. Holland had not cried since she could remember. She knew how to fight back tears quickly, hating the weakness she felt when they came. She knew how to fight sadness with anger. But her ability to fight deserted her, melted in the hot sun.

Luke sat by her side and put his arm around her, not saying anything. Only making her cry harder. Holland realized once again, Luke was the kind of person that didn't even feel angry at how she had just treated him, making him leave the pool when he was enjoying it, telling him to shut up. Luke didn't hold that against her. He was just so nice that he sat by her on the main street curb, and put his arm around her and tried to comfort, which only made Holland that much more aware of the kind of person she was.

She wondered if she would end up like her mom. Except instead of being filled with sadness, she would always be filled with anger.

Holland cried for a long time, sitting in the hot Arizona sun, with her brother's sweaty little arm around her. When she finally cried herself out, and became coherent enough to realize where she was sitting, with a face that must look unquestionably as red as her hair, she became embarrassed.

Holland looked over at her brother who sat with a face

that had grown red because of the heat, but showed a look of tenderness and concern. Holland wondered if tomorrow, when he started fifth grade, he would get eaten alive in such a crappy town. She shuddered again, and smiled wanly.

"Thanks, Luke," it seemed feeble.

Just then, Holland looked up at a red pick-up driving by. Three people sat in the cab. At the passenger window a Native American boy sat staring out of the rolled-down window. He seemed almost within touching distance, the pickup moving slowly. Holland had time to really look at him. He was incredibly handsome. His black hair, cut so short, it poked up like sticks. His dark eyes studied her with kindness. Then the next second, he looked down in embarrassment, like he happened on a private scene.

Chapter Seven

Lawrence jittered with anxiety. He could not remember ever feeling fear this strong. He was starting Holbrook High School the next day and living away from home for the first time in the Indian dormitory. His family had even hired the medicine man to perform a ceremony of protection for him.

Earlier that morning Lawrence said his good byes. He and his mother and father walked down to his grandparent's hogan. After more time and emotion than made him feel comfortable, he still had to go next door to his Auntie Red and Uncle Tilden's. Still after a few more uncomfortable good byes and ruffling the hair on his cousins' heads too many times, he finally managed to make it outside.

His mother went back into the house for the last few

things while Lawrence and his father stood by the pickup. Lawrence felt panic surge through him. He wondered if he should just go to Many Farms High School, and live at home. Maybe going to Holbrook to live in the dorms was not such a good idea. Maybe he was making a big mistake.

His father seemed to read his mind, "Lawrence it is a good and right thing you are doing. Do not question it."

Lawrence tried to smile, but could not and bowed his head. His father put his hand on Lawrence's shoulder and continued, "It will be hard for a few weeks. You will feel homesick, but concentrate on your academics and the rest will fall in place. Whatever you do, do not let your homesickness get in the way of school."

Lawrence could only nod. He and his parents climbed into the red Ford and drove slowly down the dirt road to the highway.

Every time Lawrence looked at his mother her eyes clouded over and she ducked her head, as if he could somehow miss the tears. He turned to look out the window at the cedars and sagebrush and wonder again why on Earth he was going to school in Holbrook. His hands shook and it felt hard to breath.

Lawrence thought about last May, when he graduated from eighth grade. Graduating as the Junior High valedictorian, he sat on the stand, waiting to give his speech. He felt extremely warm under his heavy, traditional, velvet shirt and turquoise necklace.

His heart stopped when he saw her. He had not known she was coming, but in the audience sat Melody and her mother, Nascha. It had been a year since he had seen Melody. Her long black hair shone like polished stone in the sun. Her eyes dancing, she smiled up at Lawrence.

Lawrence remembered when Melody left with her mom, left for good. Melody was always in trouble at school, always picking on and fighting someone. But Lawrence never fought with her.

Before they started school they spent their days playing in the sandy wash near their homes.

With a smile, Lawrence remembered the cities and stories they had built in the sand of the wash with the rusted Tonka dump trucks, stick-people, and whatever else was at hand.

When they started school, Melody was a bully. Lawrence felt sorry for the other kids. With ease Melody took over and established herself as queen bee of the pecking order. He knew everyone hated her, but would put up with her so they did not become her next target.

Lawrence kept one eye on Melody, and would swoop in and try to remove her from a situation before it came to fists. Usually he succeeded. He knew how to prevent Melody from pulling the wool over his eyes. He had always understood it clearly.

And then it happened. Lawrence remembered exactly when he changed his mind and understood that Melody could have power over him, a lot of power. And that he should never allow that.

It was in October, of sixth grade, when Lawrence quit taking care of Melody. One day during Navajo language class, Melody cheated and got caught. Melody claimed that she and Lawrence copied off each other.

The teacher, Mrs. Yazzie, loved Lawrence for the excellent student he was and doubted the story, but knew how he helped Melody stay out of trouble. They each received a week of lunch detention. The next day when they took their lunches to the detention room, the supervising teacher left for a few minutes.

Melody immediately started talking to the other kids in detention, "Did you guys know that Lawrence the Great is in lunch detention for the first time? Lawrence, so how does it feel to come down from your perfect world and become one of us?"

Lawrence studied Melody with her teasing smile, and felt a shift within him that he had never before felt. He gazed at her hair hanging to her waist, her brown eyes, her scornful smile, and did not understand his reaction. He did not understand the attraction that welled up within him. He did not understand how Melody, his friend since practically birth, could make him feel this kind of a desire for her.

The teacher returned and everyone went quiet. Lawrence sat with his heart pounding in his chest, struggling to understand how he could feel that intensely for Melody. It angered him and he vowed that he would not go through life allowing anyone, especially someone like Melody, possess any power over him.

Soon after the detention experience, Melody's mother,

Nascha, came for Melody. Nascha had remained sober for several months and the tribe granted back custody.

Lawrence felt relieved to have Melody gone, to not deal with his intense emotions for her, but he missed her. He remembered sitting on the stand during his graduation. He had known for sure the feelings were still there. He felt them as strong as ever. It shocked him that a girl, so completely differ-ent than him, could evoke that strong of a draw.

Chapter Eight

Lawrence, Lawrence. Did you go somewhere?" His mother was laughing, looking at him curiously.

Lawrence smiled, glad to see his mother laughing.

His nervousness peaked as they pulled into Holbrook. Driving down Main Street, Lawrence felt sick to his stomach. He rolled down the window to stick his head out and get some air.

A few blocks ahead he saw two people sitting on the curb, a boy and a girl, their red hair gleaming in the sun, catching his eye. The girl's hair was the reddest hair Lawrence had ever seen, thick and out of control. Lawrence felt instantly distracted.

As they drove closer, Lawrence could see the girl had

been crying. The younger boy's arm hung around the girl. Her face gave her a look of vulnerability that touched Lawrence.

The girl looked up and locked eyes with Lawrence. He could see the depth of frustration written on her face. Her embarrassment when their eyes met caused Lawrence to look down. His heart drummed, and he did not know if it was because of the beautiful girl or that the dorm was a couple of blocks away.

As they pulled into the dorm parking lot, Lawrence glanced across the street at the high school. It looked large and cold. He swallowed hard. It felt like the most idiotic thing he had ever done, coming to Holbrook High School. He wondered again why he was doing it.

Lawrence looked through the crowd and on the other side of the parking lot he caught sight of Melody and Nascha unloading. The sight of Melody brought a surge of hope to Lawrence. He wanted to make his way to her and say hi, but he did not want to tell that to his parents.

Inside the dorm entry, the four sacred mountains surrounding the Navajo reservation were depicted in tile work, giving Lawrence a small sense of relief from his nervousness.

Lawrence and his parents made it through the crowd of students and family members to his room. He would share it with one other student. The room had two bunk beds, but where the lower bunk should be, there was a desk. Shiny tile floors and a window with a curtain were the contents of the small dormitory room.

His mom sat on the chair by Lawrence's desk and bit her lip. His dad stood leaning against the door. Lawrence made a poor attempt at being cheerful, but his voice stuttered when he tried to speak, "I'll just start unpacking my things."

His hands trembled as he unzipped his suitcase and began putting the folded clothes into the drawers of the dresser.

His dad seemed to see the situation deteriorating quickly and said, "Antonia, we best be on our way."

His dad shook his hand and did something that shocked him. He kissed Lawrence on the cheek. This rare display of affection made his mom gasp, and a few tears spilled down her cheeks. "Lawrence, don't forget to bring home your dirty clothes. This weekend we could go to Chinle to the rodeo," she sounded like she was fighting to keep her voice steady as she embraced Lawrence.

With his dad pulling on her arm, they left Lawrence alone in his room. Lawrence moaned within himself. It felt much harder than he dreamed it would. Part of him wanted to run down the hall and beg his parents to take him home, but another part of him steadied himself. He took a deep breath and stared at the floor.

A bag thrown against the door made Lawrence jump and he looked up to meet his roommate, Cody John, as he came banging in. Cody, Lawrence had heard, was a reservation cowboy and bull rider.

He greeted Lawrence with a contagious smile and handshake. He spoke loudly. "Can you believe it? They put the smart-ass and the dumb-ass together!"

His humor disconcerted Lawrence, "I'm really not all that smart." The words actually sounded about right.

"Oh get off it you idiot. Everyone knows you're a brain and everyone knows I am the best damn cowboy from the Navajo reservation!"

Lawrence smiled nervously. Cody tackled Lawrence to the floor and sat on him and pounded his chest, "This is called

Indian torture. Have you ever been Indian tortured by an Indian before?"

"Yes, yes, you're crazy!" Lawrence squirmed to get away, laughing so hard he could hardly talk. Lawrence turned his face to see Melody and Nascha standing in the doorway. Melody watched the scene with an unsure half-smile.

Cody looked up at the same time and spoke before he thought, "Whoa, who the heck is that?"

"Uh, hi, Melody. Hello, Mrs. Begaye," was all Lawrence could think of, his face flushing.

Cody jumped off Lawrence, and stood next to Melody, smiling a little too big, shaking mother and daughter's hands vigorously.

Melody looked at Cody and smiled, then immediately looked back to him, still on the floor, his heart pounding.

Cody butted in, a little more composed, "I'm Cody. If there is anything you need, anything at all, I'm your man," Nascha studied Cody dubiously, and smiled.

Melody made a face at Lawrence and said before leaving, "See you around."

When Melody and Nascha were gone, Cody exclaimed, "Holy moly crap, who was that?"

"It's my cousin, well she is not really my cousin, but we sort of grew up together," Lawrence felt embarrassed.

"Well is she your cousin or not?" Cody demanded.

Lawrence knew exactly what he was getting at and replied firmly, "No, she is not. Her mom is my mom's sister's husband, so I guess we are not blood relatives but we have been like cousins growing up. My aunt and uncle mostly raised her."

"Well, it is obvious you have the hots for her and can't say that I blame you. She is one pretty little mama," Cody answered, matter-of-fact.

"No, I really don't have the hots for her." Lawrence replied defensively. "She has been trouble as long as I can remember . . . I mean, not trouble really. She's actually a ton of fun, but . . ." Lawrence squirmed in his boots.

Lawrence breathed a sigh of relief when he was interrupted by the intercom calling students to meet in the dining room. Cody laughed at Lawrence's explanation and punched him, almost knocking him over, as they left the room to the meeting. Lawrence was anxious to find Melody in the swarm of students.

Through the noise and congestion, Melody and her mom worked their way to the girls' side of the dorm.

Nascha spoke loudly over the noise, "You okay honey?"

"Fine," Melody replied with fake cheerfulness.

"It will be nice to have Lawrence here," Nascha yelled over the noise of all the students finding their rooms.

"Probably already arranged a meeting with the principal, to tell him what could be done to improve the school," Melody likewise raised her voice, cynically. She wrinkled her nose, both at the thought of Lawrence's meeting and the smell of the dorm, like a bottle of pine-sol.

Her mom laughed, "Oh, Melody, cut the poor guy some slack. He is probably as uptight as you today."

"Yeah, right!" Melody sighed. Lawrence had not looked uptight just then while she had been scared and nervous all day. Just as she had expected everyone would love Lawrence, and he would get along easily with everyone, and everyone would admire and respect him.

Melody shivered, shaking her head, while she . . . the girls would probably all hate her. The boys, who did give her the time of the day, would not like her in the way she wanted to be liked. The feelings overwhelmed Melody. She felt a strong urge to talk to Lawrence, so he could comfort her, and an equally strong urge to never talk to him again.

She put away her thoughts and searched for her room number, "Here it is!" They entered a room identical to Lawrence's. "Wonder where my roommate is?"

"Maybe they have heard of you and decided not to give you one," Nascha teased, but then seeing the worried look on Melody's face she added, "She will be here. Just be patient."

"Mom you know I can do this," Melody demanded.

"Yes, I sure do," Nascha smiled. "But you know I will be lonely without you."

"Mom, be careful and take care of yourself and call me anytime you need to," Melody looked suddenly worried while scrutinizing her mom.

Nascha looked straight into Melody's eyes and firmly said, "Melody don't you worry about that. I will be okay. I am staying strong."

"I'll see you Mom," Melody answered almost giddy.

"Love you," Nascha answered quietly and left the

room.

Chapter Nine

Melody sat on the chair, waiting for her roommate. When no one came she shrugged her shoulders and started unpacking. After a few minutes an announcement came over the intercom for everyone to meet in the dining hall, for a short meeting before dinner.

Melody walked in the crowd alone to the dining hall She quickly scanned the room, and caught sight of Lawrence across the room. Melody's breath quickened and she berated herself for being so excited to see him. After all, it had only been a few minutes.

Cleo Thomas, the dorm director, stood before the students, "Students, may I have your attention. We have a few details to attend to before supper. We welcome you to Tiisyatin

Dormitory. We hope your stay here will be a great experience. As you know, we are quite strict about our rules. We have one hundred and twenty students and we cannot have chaos going on. Your parents have entrusted you to us during the week and we take that trust seriously."

As Mrs. Thomas went through the list of rules, Melody continued to stare at Lawrence. She thought about a few weeks before, of the kiss, and then of him saying it was crazy. It sure didn't feel crazy to her.

As if feeling her eyes on him, Lawrence turned his head to look straight at her, as if he knew all along exactly where she stood. He smiled shyly. Melody flustered and looked down for a few seconds before glancing back up to see Lawrence had turned back to Mrs. Thomas.

Melody tried to act interested in Mrs. Thomas's continued instructions. When she finally got the courage to look again, Lawrence glanced back at her and smiled again.

Then Mrs. Thomas said something that made the entire group of students listen, "Many of you have heard about the train accident a few weeks ago. Please, we want all of you to stay away from the tracks. Many rumors are flying, most of which I am sure are untrue."

Melody wondered what rumors were flying. She had heard of the train wreck, but not of any rumors.

After the meeting, the swarm of students began making their way to the dining hall. Melody hung back a few minutes glancing over at Lawrence.

She saw Cody punch Lawrence in the arm, and say something Lawrence nodded and left with him. Melody watched him get in line, feeling slightly deflated, but she squared back her shoulders and got in line, feeling hungry.

The dining hall was crowded and loud. Melody filled her tray and glanced around for Lawrence, but she had lost sight of him, so she started to make her way back through the crowd toward an empty seat.

Suddenly, a girl Melody bullied relentlessly in elementary school stood glaring into Melody's face. Toshee had grown much larger than Melody, and stood a good three inches taller, with a small hunch. Her heavy belly breathed tight behind her T-shirt.

"Well, look what scum Holbrook High School admitted," Toshee said with an angry glare.

Melody was caught off guard. She relived the times she tried to scare Toshee to death and even physically tormented her. Melody felt embarrassed and yet angry at the same time.

"Hi, Toshee," Melody stuttered. "Hey . . . let's just let bygones be, well, gone."

"Yeah right!" Toshee snarled with building anger. "You made my life hell. But you know what Melody, I am not afraid of you now, and I would just as soon pound you as not."

Melody sized Toshee up and knew it was probably true. She knew her only hope would be fear. Melody felt completely annoyed by the threat.

She put her tray down and stepped right into Toshee's face, "Just give it a try," she said calmly.

Toshee stepped back, dismayed at Melody's boldness. She snarled, "You're still the creep you have always been. You just better watch your back." With that she stomped off, several girls leaving with her. They each gave Melody snide, ugly smiles. Melody found a seat, and sat shaking. She decided she probably had that coming. But determined she would never be afraid of them or anyone.

Chapter Ten

The night before the first day of school Holland lay in bed feeling pure fear. Not fear for going to school for she excelled in school, but fear of a new school, in a new town, surrounded by Native Americans.

She finally fell asleep and had one of her dreams. Some of her dreams were of an incident that had already taken place, like remembering everything in detail. A few times, when she had dreams of things that had not happened, within a day or two, things happened just like she dreamed. She could never tell anyone about those, those dreams telling her the future gave her the creeps.

This dream was of something that happened before. She was a little girl. She had walked into her parent's bedroom to find her mother sobbing on the bed. Her dad was sitting next to her, stroking her hair, trying to comfort her. It was the first time Holland recalled recognizing the emotion of fear.

Holland watched her dad try for several moments to comfort her mother. When he could not, Holland could see the anger in him grow. She somehow understood that he was angry because he could neither do nor say anything that seemed to help. Finally, in frustration, he stomped out of the room, grabbing Holland's hand and pulling her out with him.

Holland felt herself moaning in the dream, trying to get out by waking up, but it went on to another experience of her past. It was a day her mother and father took the family for a day at the beach. The weather was perfect. Dad set up an umbrella and the family ate lunch under it. Holland and Luke played in the waves, running, and laughing. To Holland life seemed perfect.

Walking back to the umbrella, Holland saw her mother lying on the picnic blanket, sobbing to her father, "I should feel happy on a day like today. I should feel happy."

Holland stood watching, fearful again, unable to make sense of her mother's words.

Her dad finally noticed her and got nervous, almost jumpy. That was the first time Holland saw him plaster on the fake Smile of Optimism. He jumped up, much too peppy-like, and took her hand, dragging her away to make a sand castle.

It was all weird and fake. She felt like telling them, but didn't. Holland knew things were wrong, were bad for her mom and it wasn't the time to act like everything was okay, because surely it was not. Holland saw and felt all of it, but didn't know what to say or how to express it. And because her dad was trying so hard, it made Holland even more nervous. So she made a sandcastle with her dad and Luke and tried to fake it also.

Holland's moaning finally woke her and took her from her dream. She wondered if she woke anyone, but everything stayed quiet. She thought about the dreams, about how the family had gone on, plowed ahead in spite of the complete weirdness of depression.

Before the move, before the hate took over, Holland found a quote in the newspaper from the author, Agatha Christie. She liked it so much she started checking Christie books out of the library.

"I like living. I have sometimes been wildly,

despairingly, acutely miserable, but through I

all I still know quite certainly that just to be

alive is a grand thing."

Lying in bed, filled with fear for school starting the next

day, battling the never-ending onslaught of hate, Holland fought

for that belief. Even, when completely miserable with all the

dysfunction, she still knew to be alive was a grand thing. She

wondered if her mother had lost that knowledge.

Chapter Eleven

The first morning of school Holland and Luke got up bright and early. Their mom did not get up, but watched them get ready for school. Weirdly enough, just the fact that she watched Holland and Luke and did not face the wall, made the day seem important.

Holland finally came out of the bathroom. She tried several things with her hair, and felt unhappy with every result. She finally just pulled it back in a ponytail.

"I'm starting high school," Holland said quietly to herself. She had looked forward to this day ever since she could remember. The complete irony of it all was that it was taking place in Holbrook, Arizona. A place she had not even heard of until a few months ago.

She should be in California, at a beautiful school, with all her friends, savoring her new jeans and cool sneakers. But instead she was living in the middle of biggest dirt pile on planet Earth, getting ready in a teepee, with her out-of-it mom lying in bed watching.

Holland was starting high school in the armpit of Arizona, going to a school that was sixty seven percent Native American. She learned the actual statistic a few days before when, after work, her dad took her to the high school to register. Holland decided on her second trip to the school that she would just describe the high school as the armpit of Holbrook.

Her dad, in his optimistic way, struck up a conversation with the principal. By listening in, Holland gained a lot of information. The whole school situation appeared absolutely nothing to be optimistic about. Holland registered for every advanced placement class offered for freshmen. She even registered to take Navajo as a foreign language.

Starting the first day of school, Holland felt sick to her stomach with fear. Her fear even trumped her anger and she wondered which emotion hurt more to feel. Holland's fear for Luke was even heavier. She thought about the previous day, at the pool, how he found a friend easily, and tried to worry less. Luke looked more like a third-grader than a fifth-grader, which brought new worry, for the hundredth time that morning.

When they were finally ready, Holland and Luke left their dad smiling broadly as he drove off to his job, and left their mother in bed. Holland walked Luke to his school. Luke, quieter than usual, didn't act as scared as she felt. She gave him the same instructions she had given him twice a day for the past week, "If anyone gives you any trouble size them up. If you think you can, beat the crap out of them. If they look too big, run fast." Luke smiled, and they both knew he wouldn't follow either instruction.

Holland hugged him tight and he gave the first instructions he had given her for school. He told her simply to act nice and everyone would like her. Holland swallowed a lump in her dry, nervous throat. Most kids are embarrassed by a sibling, and especially a hug from a sibling. Holland realized she and Luke had never been in that category, would never be in that category.

Holland walked to the high school. She tried not to think about the fact she did not know one single person in the school. The possibility of being a minority in school, never before crossed Holland's mind. She tried not to think, but her brain whirled like a windmill pushed by an exceptionally strong wind, the kind that blew right there in northeastern Arizona.

Trembling inside, Holland walked down the hall toward her first class. She carefully navigated her way through a sea of brown. Her red hair burned. Hundreds of dark eyes took a double take.

Holland searched the jam of people, in the hall, for one light-haired head, and did not see one. It sent her jitters over the top, and she started talking to herself. "You can do this Holland. That's right keep on walking, just a little ways further."

A few students noticed and smirked at her, making her aware of it. Her embarrassment crushed over the nervousness and she quit talking.

She stumbled into her first-hour class, advanced placement English. She fumbled to a desk in the back row, grateful to collapse and heave her backpack on the desk. Biting her lip to keep from talking to herself, she sat on her hands so no one could see them shaking. She worried that if anyone even looked at her she would burst into tears.

The teacher called the class to order. Holland took a few deep breaths and scanned the room. Her heart stopped. The beautiful boy from the red pickup sat a row over and a few seats up. Her face burned with the memory of when she first saw him.

Holland could only hope that he did not remember the event, or remember her. But she could not pull her eyes away from him. He looked tall, thin, and beautiful. His short, thick black hair spiked everywhere. When the teacher called roll, she said, "here" as quietly as possible, hoping he would not turn and recognize her or remember.

She found out his name was Lawrence Yellowhair. Holland thought it was a really weird name, for someone with jet-black hair.

Holland did not hear the teacher speaking. She watched Lawrence. Quickly, Holland noticed something. Lawrence sat watching someone as intensely as she watched him, a girl a few rows in front of him. The girl had long, straight hair, the exact color as his.

The girl looked athletic, which was the first strike, for Holland, against her. Holland was not athletic in the slightest, and always envious of girls who were.

Holland couldn't believe it. She felt jealous of the girl because Lawrence sat looking at her. Holland felt flooded and sick of the intensity of her emotions, sick of feeling so strongly about everything. She tried not to watch him.

The teacher spoke to the girl and called her by name, Melody Begaye. "What is with these names?" Holland mumbled angrily. As hard as she tried, she could not stop herself. She watched Lawrence watch Melody the rest of class. Holland hoped she would not have other classes with him, and then hoped that she would.

The class finally ended. The girl, Melody, immediately went to Lawrence and they started comparing schedules. Holland tore herself away and made her way to her next class, advanced-placement Biology. Remembering her misery in first-hour she walked to the front of the class and sat at a lab table with two stools.

The next minute, she caught her breath. The boy, Lawrence, sat on the stool next to her, looking a little nervous himself. She felt paralyzed and knew the warmth of her face showed. Holland searched her mind wildly for something clever to say.

Lawrence turned to her, "Hi."

Holland stuttered back, "H-hi," Wincing inside, knowing her face went completely red, worried she looked like a sunburned idiot.

Holland looked around the classroom, mainly so she did not have to look Lawrence in the eyes acting so idiot like. She didn't see Melody in the class. Holland desperately wanted to talk to Lawrence, but could not mutter a single word.

A few minutes later, the teacher called roll. When Holland's name was called, Lawrence looked over at her and smiled again. Holland felt her face burn hotter, with what she felt sure was a deeper shade of red.

The Biology teacher, Mrs. Ballard, talked for a few minutes about what the class would entail. The teacher was young, and obviously enthusiastic about her subject.

"Students, pick a lab partner, someone you could work with for the school year." A few of the students moved to different tables. Lawrence didn't move, and a nice swimming pool filled with California kids could not have pulled Holland away.

The teacher explained that the lab partners needed to

get to know one another, so she had made up questions for them to ask.

Mrs. Ballard passed out the handout to each lab table. Holland felt her heart swell with a love for this Biology class. It became her new favorite.

Holland's voice shook as she asked the first question, but she gathered her courage to look Lawrence in the eyes, "Umm, Lawrence, are you a Holbrook native?"

Lawrence smiled a beautiful smile. His voice sounded surprisingly quiet and steady, "No, Holland, I live on the reservation, near Chinle."

"Chinle?" she asked.

"It is a couple of hours north of here, on the reservation. You know what the reservation is?" Lawrence asked, half-kidding, half-serious.

"I know what Indian reservations are."

"Have you ever been on one?" he asked.

Holland remembered a field trip in California, "I've been to the Shoshone reservation. Maybe I've driven through others, and didn't know it," Holland felt lighter than she had in months.

"How about you? Where are you from?" Lawrence

asked, looking at Holland's hair in a way that made her heart skip.

"California," was her only answer. Holland dearly wished she was clever in conversation. "Have you ever been on one? California that is?" Holland asked all mumble jumble like.

Lawrence smiled at her stupid, stupid stumble, but she didn't get the impression he laughed at her, "No, I've never been on a California."

Holland flushed again, "Have you ever been in California?"

"Really, never been in California," he responded.

"So, what are you doing here?" Lawrence asked. Then his voice grew quiet. "Can I ask you something?" And then before she could even answer, "Why were you crying on the curb?"

Lawrence's frankness and kind manner unnerved Holland. She didn't know how to reply. She bit her lip and searched her mind for some kind of answer that did not make her sound as bad as she was.

"Just one of those days, huh?" he simply asked.

Holland nodded, breathing relief. They both smiled.

Lawrence asked the next question from the list, "What is your favorite subject?"

Holland wondered if she should tell him and get it over with. She loved school, got an A in every class, and did whatever work it took for top grades. Most guys were not impressed with that information, and Holland had been called everything from a brown-noser to a grade-grubber.

She decided to just get it over with and tell him, "Actually, I love school. I think Biology is my favorite subject."

To her great relief, Lawrence seemed genuinely impressed.

"I am a great believer in education," Lawrence said, talking like he was about ten years older than he was, making her laugh.

She immediately corrected her mistake when Lawrence's eyes clouded for an instant, "No, really, I totally get that. I feel the same way about education."

Lawrence asked another question, "Where do you live?"

She hesitated but figured it was going well so far. "I live

in a teepee on Main Street. Our house was supposed to be ready by now, but well, you know, things don't always go as planned," Holland cringed at her words.

Lawrence smiled at Holland, "Well technically, it is not a teepee, but a wigwam. Navajos live in hogans. But I live in a house. My grandparents live in a hogan."

Her mind was swimming with the information. Lawrence seemed from a world so far removed from hers, but she had never talked with a guy so easily in her life.

"What exactly is a hogan?" she asked.

"It's a home, which has one large room. It is usually octagonal, made of logs, with a mud roof. There is a wood stove in the middle for heat in the winter."

The rest of the hour went far too fast, most of the time spent asking questions of each other. It was bliss. She hated for the class to end. However, to her delight, she had two other classes with him, P.E. and Navajo. The other girl, Melody, also had P.E. with Lawrence and Holland. Holland decided P.E. was not going to be near as great as biology.

In P.E. she saw that Melody was indeed an athlete. Holland could tell she would outshine all the girls and most of the boys. Holland did not speak to either Lawrence or Melody during P.E. She just watched them, taking in as much as she could about their interactions.

In Navajo, Lawrence sat behind her. Holland spent the time wishing that Lawrence was studying her as intensely as she'd studied him in first-hour.

Surprisingly, especially to Holland, at the end of her first day of school she felt content and relieved.

Luke was waiting for her at the corner of the street. She knew his school got out a full forty-five minutes before hers. It was a hot August day, and his face was beet red.

He smiled when he saw her, "How'd it go, Holland?" he asked, in a way that let Holland know he'd worried about her.

"It was good," she smiled.

"You're in a good mood!" Luke beamed. "I like my teacher and I found a friend, a kid named Cordell. They teased me about my red hair. The Navajo reservation is the largest of all the Indian reservations," It all tumbled out of Luke quickly, like he had to make good use of her happiness before it evaporated.

"Well aren't you getting into Navajos," Holland teased,

feeling guilty about how hard she must have been to live with the past few weeks.

"They talk kind of funny and they have weird names, but I really like them," Luke replied enthusiastically.

Holland couldn't help but agree. Luke's voice suddenly grew serious, "Holland, a kid at school was talking about the train wreck, about the man, why he did it." Luke's eyes grew wide with worry.

"Luke do you think he really knows or do think he just talked to talk?" She didn't want to come down from her high, didn't want to talk about such horrible things, didn't want to go to that place again. Holland knew Luke wanted to talk about it, and promised herself that she would. Soon.

Luke shrugged his shoulders. They walked home and went to that place anyway. They walked in the wigwam to find their mother still in bed, with red, blotchy eyes.

Chapter Twelve

The next day in P.E., Lawrence made sure to stand where he did not have Melody in his sights. The good-looking red-haired girl, Holland, was also in P.E. Lawrence could have guessed, but seeing Holland warm up for softball, he could see quickly that she was not athletic. He kind-of liked her more for that. Melody was always very competitive and by far the best girl athlete in the class.

He couldn't help but notice that the other boys in the class acted very friendly towards Melody, clamoring to be around her, while most of the girls did not seem to give her the time of day.

Lawrence was on the opposite team of Holland and Melody. Melody was the pitcher, but she could have easily played any position on the field and dominated. Holland ended up in right field, less chance of a ball going there.

Unfortunately, the first hit from the first batter was a fly ball, straight to right field, straight to Holland. Lawrence watched from the dugout as the ball landed smack in Holland's glove. Holland did not have to step to the right or the left, the softball dropped neatly into her glove. Even from the dugout Lawrence could see the look of surprise on her face and then, a split second after it landed, the ball rolled out of her glove and onto the ground.

Lawrence could see Holland's cheeks immediately burn red and he could not stop himself from smiling. The skinny girl with pink cheeks looked completely cute. Melody turned to Holland with a glare on her face. He felt sorry for Holland. She would have Melody's wrath.

When the inning finally ended, Lawrence headed for first base. Holland walked dejectedly past him. Her cheeks glowed again as she met his eyes. Lawrence laughed and grabbed her thick mop of a pony tail and gave it a tug. Holland instantly smiled and shrugged her shoulders.

As Holland walked to her dugout, Lawrence watched

Melody, who stood staring at Holland with a puzzled, hard look.

When Holland's turn to bat came, she walked to home base and looked like the bat felt much too large for her to lift, let alone swing. Holland hit a little blooper straight to Lawrence. He reluctantly stepped on the base right before she reached it.

Lawrence put his hand on her shoulder and said he was sorry. Holland smiled even bigger and, once again, her cheeks burned red. He wondered if she ever felt any emotion without red on her face.

As Holland returned to the bench, Lawrence noticed again Melody's hard glare, taking in their every interaction. Holland returned her look, confused. A look as if she wondered if they were boyfriend and girlfriend, or if they had been in the past.

He could see her curiosity at where the intense hostility from Melody came from, when they had not spoken a word to each other. He saw the questions piling up behind Holland's eyes.

Chapter Thirteen

Walking across the street from the school to the dorm after the second day of school, Melody's thoughts were jumbled. She had watched Lawrence and the red-haired girl in P.E. smiling and looking at each other. It frustrated the hell out of her.

She wondered what in the world he could see in the girl. She looked pale and skinny and possessed no athletic ability, not an ounce. Her red hair was like a tangled bush, thick and snarled.

No getting around it though, the girl lit up like a Christmas tree whenever she spoke with Lawrence. And frustratingly, Lawrence also lit up.

Melody sat outside the dorm on a small bench, trying

to sort out her thoughts. She wondered why she had not been assigned a roommate, wondering how much her reputation had preceded her.

She thought about the reasons Toshee hated her, and wondered if Toshee would try to do anything to her. She thought about what she already felt like doing to the red-haired girl. She jumped a little when from behind a boy leaned in close and put his arm around her.

"Hey, here is a good looking girl," The boy said way too smoothly.

Melody was not quite sure how she knew who he was, but she did. She knew he was Troy Littleben, an eleventh grader. His popularity abounded far and wide at the school. He played football as well as basketball, and on the Navajo reservation, and in the town of Holbrook, basketball reigned supreme.

Melody felt too stunned to answer. She squirmed out of his grasp, and stood up to face him.

"Who are you?" Melody demanded, not willing to give him the pleasure that she already knew.

"You don't know who I am?" Troy immediately seemed

embarrassed at the way it came out.

Melody immediately picked up on his embarrassment, noticing Troy's good looks, and definite arrogance. He was only a little taller than she was, with a stocky, muscular build. His letterman's jacket plastered with letters.

He was too smooth to not recover quickly. He started talking again, "I saw you at a hoop shoot contest in Window Rock a couple of years ago."

"Yeah, I won," Melody said simply.

Troy laughed, "You did some really good shooting. I told you so after the contest. Do you remember that?"

Melody shook her head and rolled her eyes, as she turned to walk in the dorm. "Sure don't."

"He seems to think he is somebody!" Melody said quietly to herself and giggled as she walked to her room.

Like a bad case of self-fulfilling prophecy, that night in the dinner line, Toshee walked past Melody and shoved her as she went past. Melody nearly fell over. Melody quickly left the line and took two large steps to catch up with Toshee.

"If you have a problem, let's just settle it right now," Melody hissed, grabbing Toshee's arm and swinging her around to face her. "Toshee you went from being a chicken to being a bully! I liked you better as a chicken," Melody chided.

Toshee went green with anger at the accusation. "You . . . You're the bully here!"

"Yes," Melody agreed. "I was a bully, and I'm trying awfully hard not to be one now, but I will tell you this only once. I am not afraid of you and I never will be, so leave me alone!"

Toshee's fear was written on her face.

Melody continued, "I don't blame you for hating me. I treated you badly, but I just want to move on. You leave me alone and I'll leave you alone."

Toshee stood blinking, shocked and scrambling for face, "You just watch, make sure you are not alone. I will find you some place, sometime, and take care of you." Toshee sputtered.

"You even touch me and I will find you and your friends and take care of all of you!" Melody answered back calmly. Her eyes on fire.

Toshee sneered and pushed past Melody, walking away with a menacing look.

Melody made her way to an empty table and sat down.

She wanted to glance over at Toshee, but stopped herself, fighting to act calm.

When Melody finally calmed down enough to notice many of the students sat staring at her. The unwanted attention, after she had fought so hard to stay out of trouble for the past few years, was more than she could take.

She felt anger surge through her veins. She stood up and threw her tray to the floor, food flying and causing a loud clatter. Immediately the whole lunchroom grew silent. Her eyes grazed over Lawrence who sat, watching in alarm. Toshee's head whipped around in shock, as she saw Melody walking towards her, her eyes opened wide.

Melody felt a strong hand grab her arm. She instantly felt relief that Lawrence had come, that he got involved with her problem. She turned around to face him, but it was not Lawrence. It was Troy.

"Whoa, little missy, you've got some temper there," Troy said, smiling happily. "Now this is not what you want, to be kicked out of the dorm in your first week of school. Come with me, we're getting out of here," Troy said firmly.

Melody glared at Toshee, but with Troy pulling her arm,

she left the dining room with him.

He marched Melody into the common living room area. It was empty and Troy sat Melody on one of the couches. He pulled up a chair in front of her, all the while chuckling like the whole event pleased him.

Melody could not help but to smile in return, but then remembered what made her so angry.

"That snake, Toshee!" she exploded, "threatening me like that!"

"Why would she be threatening you?" Troy asked, looking like he knew the answer.

"Umm, well," Melody stalled, embarrassed, "I umm, I used to kind of, bother her."

"Ha! I knew it!" Troy exploded.

"Knew what?" she exploded right back.

"I knew you were trouble!" he said smiling, nodding almost to himself.

Melody felt furious. "Thanks for helping me, she replied stiffly and never say that again."

"What?" Troy seemed confused.

"I am trying my hardest to not be trouble. I hate hearing

that. I hate anyone who tells me that! I am not trouble."

Melody heard how strange she sounded and a small giggle worked through her angry face. Especially when she remembered the cold stares she had been giving the red-headed girl.

Troy smiled at her, a confused smile, "Yeah, I could see back there just how much you've left trouble behind. That girl is twice as big as you and you were provoking a fight!"

"I'm not afraid of her. She's afraid of me. She should be . . . "Melody felt the contradictions of what she was trying to be and what she was.

Troy laughed, "What did you ever do to get under her skin like that?"

Melody smiled grimly, "I remember one time I told her I would get my skinwalker friend to come get her."

Troy laughed again loudly, "You said what?"

Melody smiled sheepishly, "I don't really have a skin-walker friend."

"You don't say," Troy could not stop chuckling. "I wouldn't be surprised if you had about four."

Melody frowned. "Don't say things like that."

"Oh, so it is okay for you to joke about things like that, but no one else?"

"You know we shouldn't be speaking of those things. What am I going to do about Toshee?"

Troy smiled broadly, "You just let me worry about that. I think I have something up my sleeve. But I do suggest that you leave her alone."

"I have been. I haven't even lived around her for the past two years," Melody shot back defensively.

"Okay, okay," Troy looked at her like he wondered what story was behind that.

Melody grimaced "What could you do that will make her not want to fight me? Are you sure you won't just make things worse?"

"Hey, hey," Troy put his hand on Melody's shoulder, making her blush. "Don't forget who I am. I may not have a, well, skinwalker friend, but I do have friends. You can take it to the bank that once I start out for something, I accomplish it."

"Thanks," Melody studied him, wondering what lay behind the words.

Troy escorted Melody back to her room. When they

arrived, Troy asked, "Who is your roommate?"

"I, I don't have one. They said I would be getting one, but . . ."

"Probably heard about you and no girl would room with you," Troy sounded like he thought he was the funniest man alive.

Melody looked at his handsome face, remembering her mom's words, hurt by his words. "Probably," she said coldly, and walked in her room and shut the door in his face.

Melody couldn't believe that a stupid idiot like Troy Littleben could see her worst fear and tease her about it. He wasn't smart enough to catch on to anything. But still it felt like all her fears boiled to the surface, exploding in her head.

"I'm scared I don't have a roommate because no one wanted to be my roommate. I'm scared that my mom will start drinking again. I'm scared Lawrence won't always be my friend that I can never change enough for him. I'm scared when I feel angry. The anger I feel is so strong it blows me away," Melody talked to herself grimly. "Are you happy now that you know I am afraid?" she said to no one.

Chapter Fourteen

Three weeks into school, Dad announced that at last the house was ready, so they left the wigwam. Although everyone felt miserably cramped there, it forced their mother to be in the same room. For several weeks she had existed in close proximity to everyone, always in bed and usually with her back towards the family, her face towards the wall, but in the same room.

Living in the wigwam sometimes her mother tried to wake up and talk to Holland and Luke when they came in from school. Some days she did not budge.

Sometimes, in the night, Holland could hear Dad whispering to Mother, telling her they should try another kind of medicine, or telling her about a therapist he'd heard about.

One night he even told her about a Navajo man that he worked with, who knew of a medicine man that would do a ceremony on a white person.

Holland never heard her mother reply. It boggled her mind. In all the years that this weirdness existed, Holland rarely heard her parents use the word depression. Although, when she heard them talking at night . . . well her dad talking . . . she knew they talked about it, but didn't speak openly with her or Luke about it.

Holland wondered if they thought they were somehow shielding her and Luke. She knew one thing for sure. No one in the family could be in denial about the situation. They were eating, breathing, and living depression, no question about it.

There were so many things to wonder about. Holland decided that the worst thing about it was the moronic, futile thinking of it all. Something big going on, something that impacted every day in a huge way, and never to discuss it? Nothing, nada, zip, zilch, just silence?

Depression was calling every shot in the household and every shot it called made things stranger than strange. Holland decided that the whole sickness of depression was that it called every shot, but made no sense.

Holland tried to remember when the unspoken rule of not discussing her mother's depression started. She couldn't remember it ever being different. It seemed as if the whole family lived, balanced precariously on the edge of survival and that discussing the situation openly might topple everyone over the brink.

The closest Mother ever came to discussing it with her, was when she apologized over and over, after Holland yelled at her there in the wigwam. The questions were endless and the anger always close behind. Holland wondered why Luke did not seem angry. He lived the same life, with the same circumstances. But he was clearly thriving with the move, and why not, he was genuinely nice, and genuinely nice people seem to thrive anywhere.

Moving into the house actually felt exciting. The house sat across the street from Luke's school. When Holland and Luke first walked the streets of Holbrook, it reminded her of the times they traveled to Mexico. It had shocked her to see the poverty. Holbrook wasn't quite as rough, but the small stucco homes, most with dirt lawns, and large shade trees in the yards, seemed similar.

In the new house, their mother went into her bedroom and closed the door, leaving the rest of them to get everything out of storage and into the house. It took a whole weekend to get the job done. But it did feel nice not to live out a suitcase, and to have her own room.

In the house, even though her mother had disappeared, it felt nice to have order. Holland spent time arranging her room, hanging pink curtains, organizing her computer and study area. She looked around, satisfied at the finished results.

Dad seemed genuinely into his job. At least his cheerfulness seemed more sincere to Holland. She had to admit to herself, that in the ocean of hate, a small island had come to the surface.

It seemed an island of happiness. Well not happy *happy*, but happier. Holland felt amazed to admit it to herself. It didn't make sense to her, but there it was, a small island of finding Holbrook interesting, of finding Lawrence especially interesting, even Melody and what her history with Lawrence must of been, seemed interesting.

The island felt like it floated more like a boat, but still it floated on the rough sea. Holbrook did have more than first met the eye. Every day Holland noticed new things. She noticed the colors of the high desert plateau and the colors on the hills, the sand and stones that had shades of purple, blue and gold, like strokes and layers of paint haphazardly applied. When one stood back to look, and let the sun shine on that paint for a while, it was captivating to look at. Holland thought the Navajo word would be *hozhoni.*

The next morning in Biology, while they were doing a lab experiment, Holland decided to ask Lawrence about Melody.

"You know that girl," she said hesitating, wondering what she should ask.

Lawrence smiled his beautiful smile. "Yeah, I know that girl . . . which girl? I know tons of girls."

"You know tons of girls?" Holland fell for it.

"Oh yeah, I know every girl in the dorm and probably Winslow dorm also."

Holland blushed, "No that girl, that girl, Melody."

Holland could see his instant reaction. He glanced around the room and then looked back at her. "Yes I know

Melody, very well. We were raised next door to each other."

"Oh! Wow. You must be very close," Holland said, trying to hide the dejection she felt.

Lawrence hesitated before answering, just long enough for Holland to catch on that there was more between them than she even had imagined. "Melody is probably the closest friend I've ever had," he stated.

"Oh, wow." This time Holland didn't even try to hide her dejection.

Lawrence smiled at her. "But we're not like boyfriend and girlfriend, or anything. We're just close. I know her really well. Just last night in the dining hall, I remembered that."

"Does she think you are boyfriend and girlfriend, because some of the looks I get from her . . . not that I think . . ." Holland glowed red.

Lawrence smiled again. "I don't quite know how to answer that."

"It's okay. I shouldn't have asked. It's not really my business," Holland said, looking nervously around the classroom.

"No, it's okay," Lawrence said gently, making her heart

thump.

Holland bit at her lower lip, and looked at Lawrence, not knowing what to say. She slowly quite biting her lip and broke out into a smile, and he smiled back.

Chapter Fifteen

One Monday, after school, Melody crossed the street, from the high school back to the dorm. She could feel fall in the air. The trees were starting to turn. The air was cooling down, but the sun fought to keep things warm.

Melody decided to walk up the side of the hill to a boulder she had found on the side of the football field hill. The rock had a large overhang, almost forming a cave. To her surprise Lawrence was sitting cross legged in the shade, playing in the dirt with a stick. He looked up, shocked.

Melody felt embarrassed, like she intruded, "Uh, hi Lawrence, I didn't know you would be here. When did you find this rock?"

Lawrence smiled, "I found it a few weeks ago. It's great

isn't it?" Melody sat down next to him, remembering the years in the wash. She picked up a stick and started drawing and digging in the dirt with him.

"How's school going?" she thought the question sounded stiff and formal, and inwardly cringed.

"It's going well," Lawrence answered, just as formally. "Are you happy here?"

"Yes, I like it," Melody answered, growing more at ease.

"So, I see that Troy guy hanging around you," Lawrence's eyes sparkled with mischief.

"Yeah and who couldn't miss that Holland girl giving you the google eyes every time she sees you!" Melody replied.

They laughed and dug in the dirt some more.

Lawrence grew serious, "You know Melody, you could try being nice to her. She needs friends."

Melody felt the old fury rear up, pulsing through her veins. She tried to hide the ugliness she felt. "Well it looks to me like she has one really good friend already."

Lawrence flashed his smile and like old times Melody felt the anger drain, as quickly as it came. She changed the subject.

"You know what the best smell in the whole world is? The smell that makes my mouth water, is the smell of dirt," Melody breathed deeply of the earthy smell.

Lawrence looked at Melody, "You're kidding. You like the smell of dirt? Now that is something I didn't know about you."

"I'm serious. The smell of dirt is totally the very best of all smells in the world."

"I think it means you are low in some mineral," Lawrence offered.

"It just means I like the smell of the earth," Melody laughed. "The smell when rain hits the dirt, just sends me entirely over the top," she sighed.

"Well, I'll grant you that is a good smell," Lawrence went silent for a minute. "How is your mom doing?"

"It, it was pretty rough for a few days after she . . . she felt so terrible about it . . . Melody's voice trailed off, lost in her thoughts. After a few minutes she asked. "How are your parents?"

Lawrence's eyes instantly clouded. Melody touched his

arm, "Hey, is everything all right?"

"I don't know," Lawrence blurted. "The past year my mother seemed like she was not doing so well. She seemed tired a lot. She was supposed to go to the doctor after I left for high school. A few weekends ago, I found out she went to her doctor in Winslow, and then to another doctor in Flagstaff, but my dad won't tell me why." Lawrence put is head down and stabbed at the dirt heavily.

"Wow, that does sound a little scary," Melody admitted.

"What scares me more than anything is my dad being secretive about it."

"I bet she will be okay," she offered, even though inside she felt worried. "Your mom is a really strong, good person. When I was little, living with Auntie Red, I always wished your mom was my mom."

"Why?" Lawrence asked.

"I was always getting into trouble, so Auntie Red would have to discipline me, and your mom always seemed so kind and patient," Melody confessed.

"Well she could give me the what-for sometimes," Lawrence smiled.

"Your mom is probably the best person I know, but Auntie Red is a pretty darn good person also. She put up with me for a long time, from when I was four months old till sixth grade."

"Well, I am sure she is happy with you now."

"Do you think so? I would be happy if I thought that were true," she smiled warmly.

Lawrence inexplicably got nervous and said flatly, "Well, I better go, especially before your football friend comes to practice."

With that he stood up and left, leaving Melody confused. One minute they were having a great conversation, the next minute, he acted uptight and left.

She sat digging in the dirt, taking in deep breathes, wondering about it all.

Melody remembered the many years she lived next door to Lawrence, with Auntie Red and Uncle Tilden. She remembered the long days she and Lawrence played in the wash next to their homes.

They could play for hours. Melody wondered at that. She seemed to have problems with almost everyone else, sooner or later.

She remembered when her mother came for her. She had been suspended from school for beating up the principal's son. Auntie Red came and took her home. As soon as they got home, Melody bolted from the pick up and down to the wash, to avoid punishment.

Down in the wash, Melody sat in the sand for a few hours. When she could see no one was coming for her, disappointment sank in. She sat running her fingers through the sand and thought, "I hate the stupid kid at school for being such a wimp. Anyone could have, I just happened to be the one who took care of him."

Suddenly it dawned on her that Lawrence had not helped her. Lawrence, who always made sure she did not take things too far, had ignored the whole thing. Melody felt intense curiosity at why he had not.

She remembered sitting in the wash wondering about Lawrence, then her mom. At that time she had not seen her mom in three years. She remembered feeling both sadness and a slanted, hopeful view of what her mom would do for her if she were around.

Back then, Melody heard bits and pieces of information about her mom. She overheard one day that her mom had been court-ordered to rehab. Melody did not know what a rehab was, so she asked her teacher, Mrs. Yazzie. Mrs. Yazzie explained that when someone gets addicted to alcohol or drugs they go to live in a place where counselors try to teach them how to live without them.

Melody snorted in disgust at this explanation. She'd wavered between feeling sure her mom needed help from no one and confused anger that her mom would leave her to live with her auntie and uncle, and not even contact her for years at a time.

"None of this is my fault!" Melody had yelled in exasperation that day.

"Whose fault is it?" Uncle Henry had asked, as he walked towards her. The dusk had hidden his approach. Melody remembered forcing a smug smile and began the lines she had given the principal about the boy needing to be taught to be a man.

"Hey," Melody interrupted her own speech, "how come you are home on a Tuesday?"

"Because my last construction job is over and my new one does not start for a week. Now answer me, whose fault is it?"

She did not want to argue with Uncle Henry. He was a man of few words, who always treated her kindly. She enjoyed being around him.

"I don't know whose fault it is," Melody haltingly said. "I just know it is not mine."

"Melody, listen to me," Uncle Henry said gruffly.

This shocked Melody and, nervously, she sat up straight.

"I am going to tell you something I share with few people. In my childhood, my father was an alcoholic. I do not wish to go into it all, but it made my mother's and my life very hard. He caused much misery and I always felt anger towards him. Before high school I started drinking also. I felt justified in doing so because of my father's poor example. I blamed everything on him. In high school, things got worse. I began failing my classes and started getting into a lot of trouble."

Melody sat curled up with her head on her knees, running her fingers through the sand. She could not control the tears that streamed down her cheeks.

"One night things came to a head. I came home late and drunk. My father met me at the door and told me if I chose to live like that I needed to leave. I went crazy mad. I could not believe my dad felt he could tell me to leave for drinking.

"I started punching my dad. He let me hit him a couple of times, and then he put his arms around me and hugged me so I would quit swinging at him. I don't think he had ever hugged me before. He said only one thing to me."

"Please do not go down this road."

"I felt his heart at that moment. I felt his regrets and of the deepness of his addiction. I knew I was precariously close, if not already addicted, and that I could never be a casual drinker. I knew I needed to quit completely. I would succeed for a few months and then fall back. At last and mostly because I met your Auntie Antonia, have I been able to stay completely away from alcohol. It would have ruined my life."

Uncle Henry looked off into the distance as he told his story, then turned and looked down at her. "Melody, I know your mom's problems with alcohol have made your life hard. But you know what? In the end, what you do will not be her fault. What you do will be on your shoulders. It will be your doing, your choice."

Melody's tears were coming so fast she couldn't stop the sobs that came from deep within.

"Later in life my mother told me that my father's childhood was filled with heartache. He had been ripped from his family and forced into a government boarding school where the treatment was harsh. He lived many angry years and used alcohol to drown the feeling. But Melody," Uncle Henry said, lowering himself to his knees so that his eyes could be level with hers, "my father still had to make the choice to drink or not, and the choice is still your mother's and how I live is my own choice and how you are acting is yours. This is the hardest of any of life's lessons to learn."

Melody blinked back the tears, shocked at Uncle Henry's many words and shocked at his directness. He spoke to her as one adult to another. She put her head down, not able to speak. Uncle Henry did not say another word, but walked back out of the wash.

Melody could not face leaving the wash that night. Nobody fought that idea. The night grew long, and the cold moved through the air and into Melody's heart. She sat in the sandy wash and eventually, early in the morning, fell into a disturbed sleep.

Throughout the night, she woke often thinking over and over that everyone was right about her. She felt the cold, stiff and miserable, inside and out.

She felt beat down, a feeling she never before allowed herself to experience. Between her off and on sleep, the question that frustrated her most during the night, finally broke her. Why hadn't Lawrence helped her? She needed him so she could be good. Lawrence offered her hope to do right. She believed she could not make it happen on her own.

Early the next morning, a crow cawing loudly woke her. As the sun broke over the horizon she climbed out of the wash. She stretched and breathed deeply the cedar and sagebrush. She scanned the horizon and to her surprise saw a car making its way down the dirt road leaving a small cloud of dust behind.

No one came to the homestead much, and especially not early in the morning. Melody walked part way home and stood behind a cedar tree and watched. The car pulled up to Auntie Red and Uncle Tilden's home.

Her mother got out. Melody wanted to run to her mother, yet she stayed behind the tree. Nascha walked to the front door and knocked timidly. When no one answered, she knocked harder.

Uncle Tilden, her mother's brother, finally opened the door. Melody could see them talking but could not hear the conversation. After a few minutes they went inside. They left the door slightly open, so Melody ran quietly to the house and stood near the open door.

"Where is Melody?" Nascha asked.

"You don't even want to know," Tilden replied steadily.

Auntie Red must have come in the room because Melody heard her say wearily, "Hello Nascha, so you came back again."

"Hello, Red," Nascha's reply sounded strained.

"Is Melody around? I would like her to hear what I have to say," Nascha's voice trembled.

Tilden answered, "Nascha, please just speak with us for now. It is for the best."

Nascha cleared her throat. "I first apologize. It has been very wrong for me to stay away for all these years."

Melody could practically hear the shock her mother's humility caused Auntie Red and Uncle Tilden.

"Second, I give my sincere thanks for you raising Melody. I know you have loved her."

Red started sputtering, but sounded like she regained her composure and remained silent.

"And third, I am here to plead with you to consider allowing me to take Melody. I have been sober for seven months, and I feel it is time. I have permission from the tribe, but I will not go against your wishes."

Quiet filled the room for several moments. Finally, Auntie Red spoke, "Nascha, things are not going well with Melody. Yesterday the principal suspended her from school for beating up a boy, his own son. Her defiance could fill a room."

Melody rolled her eyes, then she heard her mother say, "This does not surprise me. It is my fault, and things have not been easy for her."

Red bristled, "Nascha, we have shown her every kindness. She should not be acting this way."

Nascha spoke quietly, "How could Melody possibly understand why I did what I did? It must hurt her."

Melody could take it no longer. She burst into the room. Everyone's shock registered clearly. Melody stood looking at her mother. She wanted to speak, to say something, but could not find a word.

Her mother came to her and wrapped her arms around her and held her tight. Melody cried like a baby. There was so much to say, so much to sort out, the mountain of it caused a mudslide that blocked it from happening.

An hour later, Melody's things were packed to go with her mom. She said goodbye to Auntie Red and Uncle Tilden, and Sage and Tilden Jr. It didn't seem real. She was really leaving the only home she knew.

"Nascha, uh, Mom," Melody stuttered as the car pulled slowly away, past Lawrence's house, "could you stop for a minute and wait here?"

"Sure," Nascha answered, just as nervous.

Melody bolted from the car and did not knock at Lawrence's front door. Auntie Antonia stood at the kitchen sink washing the breakfast dishes.

"Auntie, where is Lawrence?" Melody burst out.

Antonia jumped, "Why, I don't know. I guess in his

room."

Melody banged into Lawrence's room, but he was not there. Antonia followed her.

"I guess he could be in the wash," she offered.

Melody ran out of the house ignoring her mother, and raced down to the wash. Antonia followed Melody, but stopped short when she saw Nascha sitting in her car, shock clearly showing on Antonia's face.

Melody found Lawrence sitting in the sand rubbing his hand back and forth. His back faced Melody.

"Lawrence," Melody yelled too loudly.

He whipped around as Melody ran as fast as she could towards him. The sand sucked at her feet, trying to hold her back.

She plowed into him, and hugged him fiercely, startling him. Melody never had been one to show physical affection.

"My mom came. She's taking me away and I'll never see you again and I am sorry that I am so bad, but I love you and please do not remember me as bad. Remember me for all the time we spent together in this wash." Her words jumbled and crashed over him like a landslide.

"W-what?" Lawrence stammered.

"This is it," Melody said and kissed him fervently on the lips, "goodbye forever, Lawrence."

"Goodbye forever?" His face heated, but his tone sounded irritated.

"Yes! I am leaving right now with my mom."

With that she turned and ran from the wash, leaving him looking dumbfounded.

#

Melody sat under the rock remembering for a long while. It was growing dark when she unfolded her long legs and stood, feeling stiff. The football team had ended practice and was leaving the field. She walked down the hill, but before she got to the only exit, Troy grabbed her arm.

"Hey I didn't see you come up here!" He bellowed.

"Well I . . . I . . ." Melody looked up at the rock she shared with Lawrence. "I just came up here looking for my sweater. I think I left it here during P.E.," she spoke with her eyes averted from Troy's eager gaze, wondering why he acted like that.

"Well I'm glad you are here!" Troy exclaimed. "I've

been looking for you all day. I want you to go to homecoming with me!" He boomed, quite pleased to be making the request.

Melody's heart sunk. She didn't know what she had been hoping for about homecoming, just not this.

"I can't date until I am sixteen," she lied smoothly by telling him something Mormons taught in seminary, a class her mother had insisted she take to help with anger issues.

"But I am going to the dance with some friends," she finished brightly. "Be sure you ask me to dance, okay?"

With that Melody smiled sweetly, turned and ran from the field, leaving Troy watching her, in a state of disbelief.

Chapter Sixteen

In Biology, Holland worked hard to achieve her new goal of trying not to act so giddy around Lawrence. She wanted to be more demure. Holland loved that word. However, the new goal was not going so well. In fact, Holland knew she was failing miserably.

Holland imagined herself like a neon sign that lit up in his presence and started to flash. Flashing, "I'm totally, tumultuously, taken with you." Not a demure sign.

Some days Holland felt down, discouraged, and disgusted with her openness. And some days she could have cared less. It was what it was. She remembered reading an article in a magazine somewhere, that explained that women should act a little less interested, a little hard to get, if they really wanted men to crazy want them. She sure wasn't pulling that off.

Holland sat twisting her hair, concentrating hard on demure. Demure, demure, she kept repeating over and over in her head, trying to will demure into her very un-demure self.

After what seemed an eternity of demure, she glanced over at Lawrence. He sat smiling at her, seeming to read her. Lawrence saw through her attempts at demure as easily as Holland saw just how wonderful he was.

Holland blushed and Lawrence laughed quietly, acting quite entertained with the demure show. Finally, embarrassed and frustrated with her heart on her sleeve, she punched his arm. Lawrence grabbed Holland's wrist, which made her heart skip several beats.

"Don't hurt me." He faked pain. "How can I take you to homecoming, if I am injured?" He looked down at the desk, confidence vanishing.

Holland felt her heart completely come to a stop. It stopped for several seconds, then started up again beating fast and hard, swelling with utter, surging, joy. She felt her cheeks grow warm. She tried to speak but nothing came, nothing cute or witty, or even remotely close to demure.

Finally, in utter complete desperation at her thick tongue, she simply nodded yes.

#

Lawrence sat smiling at Holland as she nodded her head over and over. There was something so open about her. "So you're saying yes?" he said chuckling.

Holland still did not speak. Lawrence studied her, feeling a sudden curiosity of her past, what her life had been like before Holbrook. Her cheeks glowed pink again and she ducked her head down.

A second before she had seemed so open, but a part of her was a closed book. He could see clearly that she protected a portion of her life and held it under close wraps. He wondered what it was.

Lawrence continued to stare at her, and she glanced up at him, with a look of vulnerability and worry. Holland was the strongest student he had ever been around. She pushed herself, was never behind, always in complete control of school work.

But he could see a side to her that seemed out of control, almost like Melody. Lawrence smiled again, thinking what a random thought, making no sense. Yet when he looked at Holland again, she wore a look of desperation.

Lawrence thought of the worries he felt for his mother. Worry about things that were most likely far from the truth, yet they gave him a feeling of desperation.

"Is everything all right Holland, I mean at home?" He asked feeling embarrassed at the question. He could not miss the reaction. She closed her eyes for the briefest of a second, her face revealing her fears.

"No, I mean yes, well," she could not find the words.

"What's wrong?" he asked gently.

She closed her eyes again, shaking her head. When she opened them tears made her eyes shine and seem larger. "It's all good," she whispered, lying poorly.

Lawrence studied her for another moment, wondering if he should go on or leave it alone.

"I want to go to homecoming with you," she stated.

"I want to go to homecoming with you too," he replied.

# # #

Melody was furious and sad. Word traveled quickly that

Lawrence was taking Holland to Homecoming. The word was also out that Troy had asked Melinda Whitehorse. No one, of course, knew that Troy asked her first. Not that she cared if they did. But she wished badly that Troy had waited and asked her that day. She would have loved to go with him and let Lawrence eat rocks.

On the bus ride home Friday, Melody felt surprised when Lawrence came and sat by her on the bus. Melody wanted to give him the cold shoulder. For several moments she half way ignored him, but she could tell he was genuinely upset about something.

She lost her temper, "Lawrence, how come you are all happy-headed around that Holland girl and around me you act like a sad puppy?"

Lawrence looked stunned, "I'm happy. What are you talking about?"

She stared at him, not answering. She could see Lawrence's eyes were red. She put her arm through his and took his hand, "Lawrence is everything okay?"

"No!" Lawrence exploded, not even noticing how loudly he spoke. Melody looked nervously around at the other students, but no one was paying attention.

"Melody, I know things are not good! I can tell something big is going on. I wonder how long they are going to keep it from me."

Melody felt sick. She could tell Lawrence was on to something. He was never one for dramatics. They sat silently for several miles. Melody kept tight hold of his hand. Lawrence sat numbly looking at them.

"What are you worried about being wrong?" she asked.

"I think my mother is sick or something," Lawrence answered vaguely.

With sudden energy she said, "Hey, I have an idea. I'll get my mom to visit Auntie Red and Uncle Tilden this weekend. Maybe we can snoop around and find something, or maybe Auntie Red knows something and I can try to get it out of her!"

Lawrence looked at Melody with hopeful eyes. "Do you think you can get your mom to come over? Do you think we could figure out something?"

"She'll agree to go," Melody replied. "She tried to get me to a couple of weekends ago, but, I ah, I thought of . . ." Melody's voice went low. "I just wondered if you would even be happy to see me."

Lawrence's eyes showed a jumble of emotions, but all he said was, "Please come. I need your help."

They sat silently looking out the window.

An hour and a half later, Lawrence gently nudged Melody. She woke in a start. She had fallen asleep, leaning her head against Lawrence's arm.

Embarrassment cleared her head and warmed her face. Lawrence quickly saw this and teased. "Wow, Melody you snored and slobbered during that nap."

"Did I?" Melody asked even more embarrassed, but glad to hear him joking.

Lawrence looked at her with a smile that seemed happy and sad, and simply said, "I watched you, and no."

Chapter Seventeen

The next afternoon Lawrence sat on his porch and watched as Melody and Nascha's car drove by. He quickly walked down to the wash and in a few minutes Melody raced down.

"What's the plan?" he asked nervously.

"Are your mom and dad home?" Melody asked.

"No, they went to the grocery store in Chinle."

"Then let's go look around," she answered solemnly.

In the house they began by looking through a stack of mail. They found nothing. "Let's look in their room," she said, embarrassed. "There might be medicine or something."

He looked panic-stricken, "I've never snooped around my parent's bedroom before."

Melody tried but could not stop her smile, "Never? Oh, come on, not even looking for Christmas or birthday gifts?" she chided.

Lawrence looked at her and shook his head no.

Melody shook her head, "Wow, you really are Lawrence the Great. You missed a whole part of childhood."

Melody would have liked to keep teasing, but the worried look on Lawrence's face stopped her.

They looked under the bed, and found nothing. They looked on Antonia's nightstand, and again nothing. They opened the one small drawer. They found a small leather book, a journal.

As they sat on the edge of the bed, Lawrence, with shaking hands, opened the book. Melody could hear a vehicle pull up to the house. Her heart hammered in her chest, knowing it was his parents.

Lawrence didn't seem to notice. There were a few entries. In one of them Antonia wrote of the chemotherapy treatments that would begin in January.

They read it simultaneously and simultaneously they caught their breaths. Lawrence handed the book to her, put his head in his hands, breathing heavily. Melody sat staring at the page, then she quietly closed the book, reached over Lawrence, and put it back in the drawer. She could hear the adults talking outside, giving her the jitters.

Suddenly, Lawrence reached up and grabbed her with such force that Melody could barely breathe. He buried his head in her neck and hair and sobbed like a child.

His emotions were so strong, his sobbing so intense, it broke her heart. This was not the Lawrence that always seemed in such control of himself. Melody sat and held him close while he cried.

She could hear Antonia and Henry, and Red and Tilden talking outside the house. She felt panic stricken that they would walk in, but couldn't bring herself to tell Lawrence.

After several moments, his crying had subsided, but Lawrence did not move. Melody felt his warm tears running down her neck and under her shirt, but she remained still, holding him as tight as she could.

Finally, he backed away, but did not take his eyes off her. She wondered if he could hear his parents talking outside. Melody leaned up and tenderly kissed Lawrence on the lips. He smiled a smile that was sad and tender.

Melody felt feeble trying to comfort him. "Depending on what kind of cancer it is, it could be very curable."

Melody kept a tight grip on Lawrence. But when she felt his parents would surely walk in, she said, "Lawrence can you hear your parents and Red and Tilden outside?"

Lawrence gave her a surprised look. She knew he had not heard. "Let's go out the back door and down to the wash." Lawrence looked around in surprise, finally hearing them.

Outside it was a warm, beautiful day. Melody breathed in the sage and cedar smell deeply.

He did not take his eyes off her, but somehow did not see her.

Once down in the wash, they sat running their fingers through the sand, feeling the warm sun on their backs, not saying anything.

Melody thought about how nice the day felt, the sun not too hot, in the wash with Lawrence. It should all feel perfect, but it could not.

Finally, after what seemed a very long time, Lawrence spoke.

"Melody, I don't know if I could go on without my mother."

Melody paused a moment then replied, "Yes, Lawrence, I'm sure you could. You are strong."

"It's funny," Lawrence said. "I always thought that too. Not arrogantly, I just always felt strong. Now I don't think that. I think my mother is strong, and somehow it made me feel I was."

"Do you remember back in sixth grade, that day I got suspended? The night before my mom came and got me, and I spent the night in the wash? Did you know that your dad came down to the wash that evening and talked to me?"

"He did?" Lawrence said surprised. "What about?"

"He told me the story about how his dad used to drink."

"He's hardly talked to me about that," Lawrence replied flatly.

"That's probably because you have not needed the extra help," she said, smiling sadly. "Anyways, he said something I never forgot. I still think about it. He said that sooner or later, what I did was because of me, that I could not blame my mom forever. He told me how he blamed his actions on his dad,' but had to learn to stop."

"What does that have to do with this?" Lawrence asked, almost annoyed.

"Well, think about Lawrence. If sooner or later we can't blame our problems on our folks, then sooner or later we can't blame our strengths on them. Sooner or later we are what we are, and we have to take the blame or credit for it. Maybe you learned to be strong because you have such a good mom, and she loves you so much, but maybe now your strength is because you are Lawrence."

He bent his head and a few more tears fell to the sand.

"You know what is really crazy," Lawrence said. "I used to think you were just a lot of trouble, a lot of fun, but mostly a lot of trouble."

"I know," she said softly.

"I really did," Lawrence continued. "But right now, after today, I have to admit that you have way more going for you than I ever gave you credit for."

She flushed and nervously changed the subject. "Remember all the towns we used to build down here?"

"I remember how much you cussed," Lawrence smiled.

"My mother always worried I would take up the habit."

"Your mom can fight this, lots of people do. There's always hope," Melody said, feeling curious about what he had just said. "She worried about my influence on you?" Then in a second she teased, "Little did she know that Lawrence the Great was never influenced by me."

Lawrence studied her, saying nothing.

A few minutes later they heard Lawrence's dad walking into the wash calling their names. Lawrence looked at Melody alarmed.

"Just act casual," she said calmly.

"Hey, Dad," Lawrence called, faking casual.

"Melody," Henry answered, ignoring Lawrence, "How nice to see you," and then, not waiting for an answer, "we decided to have a cook-out at Red's. Come help us."

She easily faked nonchalant. "It is so good to see you, Uncle Henry."

As they climbed out of the wash, Henry sent them back inside to get some food items. Once inside, while Lawrence was gazing absent-minded into the fridge, he said, "My dad knows."

Melody looked at him puzzled.

"He knows I know," Lawrence repeated quietly.

"Why do you say that?"

"I think he knew as soon as he saw us."

"Wow, really? That is kind of weird. Is it kind of like ESP or something?" she asked, only half-joking.

"I think when stuff this important is going on you just kind of know some things. Like I knew something was going on, I just didn't know what for sure."

It made her nervous. "Do you know the things about me that are important too? Like how I feel about you?"

"What? What do you mean?" he looked around uneasily.

Melody looked at him, wondering if she would ever completely understand him, if he ever would even want to understand her.

Chapter Eighteen

Monday morning, Holland's mind swirled as she sat waiting for Lawrence to come into Biology. As she sat and watched him and Melody in first-hour English, she could tell for sure something had happened.

Lawrence looked tired and down, and he watched Melody with an intensity that was painfully hard for Holland to watch. She hurried from first-hour, her mind preoccupied by what she saw.

"Hi." Lawrence sat down heavily.

"Hi," she said tentatively.

"How was your weekend?" he asked formally, his mind seemingly far, far away.

"Probably better than yours," she looked inquisitively at

him.

Lawrence returned her look, quietly. He had a way of studying her and looking at her hair that always made Holland's heart pound in her ears.

He opened up his notebook, bent over and wrote something, tore out the page and pushed it over to her.

Before Holland could compose herself, and not act so eager, she smiled at him, smiled at the note. She felt herself smiling so hard that she was sure every square centimeter of her teeth showed.

Lawrence smiled back and laughed a little. He pointed to the note, "At least read it before you catch a bug."

Holland felt too happy to even feel humiliated like she should have. She opened the note.

"Would you go to the football game with me before the homecoming dance?"

Holland hardly dared look up. Homecoming was the coming weekend. For a few seconds she allowed herself to enjoy the soaring joy that pulsed literally through every cell of her body.

Lawrence watched her intently, but still had the look of

being somewhere else. Holland wondered for split second if he worried she would turn him down, but quickly released that thought. He was much too intelligent to wonder that.

"Thanks, I'd like to," Holland replied trying to tone her smile down a bit.

Lawrence sat looking at her, but not really seeing. Holland remembered how things seemed a few minutes earlier. How Lawrence acted in first hour. He surprised her by asking.

"Holland, do you have anybody that you hang out with?"

Embarrassment flooded her again. Nobody controlled the swing-shift on her emotions like he did. But what could she tell him? Should she admit that other than him, she really had not made friends with anyone? Or that she was fairly sure that the other students would not want anything to do with her. That they never asked. Or should she say that she never tried. Should she tell him that after school Luke was waiting for her and that she wouldn't have dreamed of sending him home alone to their mother?

She wondered if Lawrence noticed she never tried to befriend anyone, if he ever noticed that everyone else pretty

much just looked at her like she was a freak. She wondered if
he knew that, so far, she didn't even care, as long as she could
talk to him. Wondering all those questions must have been written on her face as much as whatever was going on with him
was written on his. They became quiet, each in their own
thoughts.

"Who do you hang out with?" he asked again.

"My little brother, Luke," she answered embarrassed.

"Is he the kid that was sitting next to you on the curb?"

Holland blushed at the remembrance. "Yes, the only
other ginger-haired kid in this town, that's my brother, Luke."

If she would have thought about it, for even a second
she would not have said it, but that seemed to be the story of
her life, saying what she thought, "That girl . . . that girl who you
know somehow, she hates my guts."

Lawrence wrinkled his face in confusion, and then realized she was talking about Melody.

"I'm sure she doesn't hate your guts," he replied un-
convincingly. His beautiful dark eyes locked with Holland's.
They both knew the truth.

Lawrence's face was so filled with thought. She flustered, "Is everything all right with you?"

He paused just long enough to let her know that he considered his answer before giving it, "Things, things are fine."

She knew he hadn't told tell her the truth and felt hurt he would not talk to her. Then she remembered everything about home she did not tell him.

Chapter Nineteen

Lawrence sat watching Holland. He somehow knew that he was only scratching the surface of her, that there was a whole story going on under her beautiful red hair and face.

He remembered first hour. He had felt so close to Melody over the weekend, and then without even planning it or thinking about it, as soon as he saw her in school he wanted to distance himself from the closeness.

The closeness almost felt threatening to him, somehow like being on shaky ground. It did not make any sense and he was in no mood to try and figure it out. As soon as he saw Holland he wanted to reach out to her. She looked like the breath of air he felt like he could not take during first hour.

He felt some relief to know about his mother, but complete apprehension. People died of cancer every day. Any time he thought of it, he felt the anxiety well up in his chest, tight and miserable.

On Sunday, before he and Melody had caught the bus to go back to Holbrook, he wanted to shout at his dad, "You know I know about mom! Why don't you talk to me about it, tell me everything you know. Why?" But the family went on, trying to act normal in a most frustrating way. He could not help but watch his mother out of the corner of his eye. He stared at her, wondering how she felt physically. How worried she was and what was going on in her mind.

A few times his mom caught him staring at her and laughed nervously, looking at his father, trying to talk about something pertaining to school. Once she asked him, "So how is it being at Holbrook High with Melody?"

The question had startled Lawrence out of his thoughts. "What? Oh well, fine I guess. I don't know."

His mother smiled, "You two always got along so well. I always thought it was sweet."

Lawrence shrugged his shoulders, "Mom, the day you and Dad took me to the dorm to start school, did you happen to notice a red headed girl and a boy sitting on the curb?"

"Where?" His mother sounded confused.

"On Main Street, right before we turned to the high school, a girl with bright red hair was sitting on the curb, um; she looked like she had been crying."

"No, I can't think of it. I don't remember."

"I saw her," his father said, surprising Lawrence.

"You did?" Lawrence felt embarrassed.

"Why?" His father asked interested.

"Well, I know her a little. I am taking her to homecoming."

"What? You didn't tell us you were going to homecoming!" His mother sounded happy.

"I guess . . . I guess I should tell you I have been nominated for attendant," he added sheepishly.

"Oh! Well, Henry, maybe we should go to the assembly."

"Melody is nominated also, but don't come, please don't come. I'd feel stupid, because I won't win."

His mother and father looked at each other.

"I mean, if you come, it will look like I expect to win or

something . . ." His voice trailed off miserably.

"What is the girl's name?" his father asked.

"Holland, Holland Adams."

"Well, that is wonderful," his mom sounded dubious.

"She moved to Holbrook from California just before school started. She has one little brother. She is really smart." Lawrence realized how little he knew about her.

"I guess I just assumed you would ask Melody." his mother smiled. "But, I'm sure if you wanted to ask this Holland, she must be wonderful."

"Yeah, I guess so. She's nice." Lawrence smiled back at his mom.

"The last of your clothes for the week are in the dryer, I'll go fold them." She left the room.

Henry sat looking at Lawrence then asked, "So why didn't you ask Melody?"

Lawrence looked at him in frustration. His father wouldn't tell him about his mom's cancer, but he would ask this? "I don't really know Dad, I just kind of like this girl."

His father looked at him and laughed softly, "Well that's a good reason."

Lawrence longed for his father to tell him everything about his mom. He sat looking at him longer than was polite in Navajo culture. His father became nervous and walked out of the house.

# # #

Holland blushed. Lawrence realized he had been staring at her while he contemplated the conversation with his parents.

"I told my parents about you," he smiled. "I told them we were going to homecoming together."

Holland's face lit up. "I told my parents that you asked me. Well I told my dad."

"Why didn't you tell your mom? I thought she lived with you," Lawrence asked, curious. He saw Holland scrambling for an answer.

"Well, yes, she lives there. I just haven't had the chance, I mean, I will." Then she changed the subject. "Were your parents okay with it?"

Lawrence studied her, wondering what she meant, wondering why she changed the subject. "Yes of course they were. My dad even remembered you from the curb."

He regretted it as soon as he said it. She bit at her lower lip, her face flushing.

"I'm so embarrassed," she whispered.

"No, no don't be." Lawrence wanted to pull her in and comfort her. "It's okay. He probably didn't even notice you had been crying. He just noticed you sitting there."

Holland took a deep breath, and seemed to steady herself. "I am really excited to go with you," she said straight forward, and so simply, that Lawrence liked her better at that moment than he had in any of the moments before.

Chapter Twenty

"Homecoming week," sighed Melody. The weekend at Lawrence's had been so emotional, she wondered how he would act now that they were back at school.

He reacted after first-hour by smiling at her, but clearly did not want to talk about anything. It stung a little. Melody wondered how Lawrence could act so close to her over the weekend and then act nervous about it.

Melody dreaded the week. Homecoming was a big deal at Holbrook High. There were activities every day. She would hate watching Lawrence and Holland together.

After school, Troy Littleben appeared at her side. She wondered how he could just show up like that.

"Coming to the game Friday?" he asked too eagerly.

Troy was the quarterback. His athleticism had elevated Holbrook's football program to a new level. Attendance at games had been very low, but lately the whole school, especially the dorm students, loved and looked forward to the games.

Melody looked at Troy. He was handsome, and all the other girls swooned over him. She wished she could feel the same.

"Sure, I'm going," she replied.

Troy always touched females excessively. It wasn't an attractive feature.

He rubbed Melody's shoulder. "Great, I'm glad you will be there. Hey after the dance a few of us are going out to the Badlands and having a bonfire."

Melody looked at Troy feeling confused, "You asked Melinda to the dance."

"Yeah, I know, but I didn't ask her to the party afterwards," Troy announced, like he was brilliant or something.

Melody wished again, his handsome face had more behind it. She wanted to like him, would have appreciated the distraction.

She couldn't think of a reply so she walked away.

The week was long and miserable. A few times Melody tried to talk to Lawrence, but he avoided her almost as if he was mad at her. It confused her. She wanted to hate his guts, but remembered what he was going through.

Melody had been nominated for freshmen girl attendant to the homecoming queen. Lawrence was nominated for boy attendant to the king.

Melody woke up Friday morning, happy that the week was almost over, but feeling cranky to have to go through the day. She lay in bed mulling over the previous weekend. It was horrible news, but Lawrence had acted so appreciative of her being there, and she'd felt so close to him. Then, bang, Monday morning he acted more stand-offish than ever.

She couldn't figure out why. Maybe it was the red-head girl. Melody saw them several times together during the week's activities, both lit up like Christmas trees. She couldn't understand his happy face, with the news he was dealing with. No girl possessed that much power.

It all seemed so weird. Melody wondered if this was his way of not dealing, if he was trying to ignore it for a week. That didn't seem like him, but she had never seen him deal with something this huge before.

She finally pulled herself out of bed, rushing not to be late for school. Instead of the usual schedule, all the students went to the gym for the homecoming assembly. The Homecoming Royalty would be announced.

Melody didn't really care that she was nominated, but suddenly in the gym, she wanted in the worst way for her and Lawrence to win, so they could stand next to each other and make Holland watch. Melody also wished, in the worst way, that she had rolled out of bed earlier and fixed up a little more.

Melody stood with the nominated girls. Lawrence stood with the other boys. The noise in the gym could not drown out hearing her heart beat loudly in her ears as the announcements were made. She won, Lawrence did not.

Lawrence smiled and winked at her as she walked past him to stand next to the queen. The queen stood next to the king, who of course was Troy. Troy grinned at her like he was trying to train his mouth to grow larger.

As the assembly dismissed Troy appeared magically at her side.

"Have you decided about tonight?"

Melody looked at him, hoping once again that he was just sweet and innocent, and dumb. She smiled as she hoped.

Troy immediately seized on it. "Yeah, you really need to. It will be fun." And before she could reply he added, "And save me some dances tonight."

Melody grimaced and Troy turned and left. It amazed her how he could carry on an entire conversation, without her saying a word.

She thought about being at a bonfire with him at the Bad Lands. She thought about the girls who would love the chance. Maybe she was misjudging him. Maybe he could be cool to hang out with.

Chapter Twenty One

Holland felt giddy when Lawrence came to the front door, politely meeting the family. Even Mom descended from her room to grace them with her presence. She actually dressed in clothes, not pajamas. It was the first time since they had arrived in Holbrook.

Even though she had dark circles under her eyes, her mom smiled sweetly at Lawrence. Dad shook his hand. Luke smiled brightly, like he could see how happy Holland was. Then they were off to the football game.

Sitting by Lawrence at the football game felt divine and just plain fun. Holland talked to him so easily. She noticed once again that Lawrence seemed a study in contrasts. He acted old and young, funny and serious, all wrapped up into one amazing package.

Lawrence leaned over to her and said, "Just so you know, I'm okay at basketball."

Holland laughed, "I could care less if you play football, or even basketball."

Lawrence looked at her, surprised, "What? I thought all girls were into athletic guys."

"You've forgotten who you're talking to. I am into smart guys and good looking guys," Holland said, thinking Lawrence looked amazingly good. Her face felt warm as she tried harder not to stare.

She composed herself and tried demure for about two point nine seconds, when Lawrence said, "Well then I should have set you up with Troy the quarterback, if you are that into looks."

 . Holland frowned. She did not know who Troy, the quarterback was. She winced inside when she immediately put two and two together and realized Troy had something to do with Melody. She glanced up behind them where Melody was sitting. Her eyes looked like they could bore a hole through her.

Holland shivered, wondering what the connection was

between them, like an invisible cord that bound them together. It filled her with despair that dissipated when she looked over at Lawrence. He smiled and took her hand.

After the game, Lawrence walked her home. He waited for her to change for the dance.

In front of the mirror, she put her new dress on. It was a deep shade of jade, more dramatic than anything she had ever worn. The bodice fit snug and flared out just above her knees. She put on her high heeled sandals, praying she did not wipe out in them. She stood up in them and knew she wouldn't pull that off, so she changed into her flat ballet shoes.

She brushed her hair and saw that her cheeks glowed, not the usual bright red of blushing, but a surprising softer shade of happiness. Standing for a minute and looking at herself, Holland realized she had never been that excited about her hair, or her looks. But standing there in that moment, she actually thought she looked pretty. Smiling at the thought, she could only hope Lawrence saw something there also. Something besides being a grade grubber, something like, a girl.

When she walked into the living room, the look on Lawrence's face let her know she looked like a girl.

Her mom and dad stood with their mouths half open. Her mom said softly, "You look beautiful Holland."

Her dad helped her into a sweater whispering, "You shouldn't be going out looking like that."

Holland smiled and hugged her dad tightly. He had been the one to take her to Flagstaff to buy the new dress, and two pairs of shoes. The ones she wanted to wear and the ones she knew she would wear.

They walked back to the dormitory and Holland waited a few minutes for Lawrence. When Lawrence came out of his room, she caught her breath. In a black suit and a tie, his black hair and white smile looked stunning.

"Um, you're beautiful," she said sincerely.

"You are too," he said, pulling her into a hug, his lips brushed the top of her forehead. It felt a little hard to breathe.

Walking across the street from the dormitory to the gym, Lawrence held Holland's hand. Holland's mind raced, wondering how, when so many things in her life could be hard and downright miserable, how simultaneously, life could be so nice, so darn nice.

Holland smiled to herself, thinking she could die that

night of food poisoning, and die completely happy.

Within two seconds of entering the gym, she thought she could feel Melody's eyes on them. Holland looked around the gym until she found her. The boys certainly liked Melody, thought Holland, watching her dance every dance. Melody was so pretty. Holland wondered for about the millionth time, about her connection to Lawrence.

Lawrence walked straight out to the dance floor. Holland was grateful it was a slow song. She was not a great dancer. Lawrence pulled her in close, "You look nervous. Aren't you having a good time?"

"No! no, I'm having a great time," she said too eagerly and tried to look like she felt.

He laughed and his mouth was close to her ear, "Holland, being around you is sweetness for me."

Holland looked up at his beautiful black eyes. It was the nicest thing she could remember anyone ever saying to her. She wondered how she could pull off any sort of demure act when he said things like that.

After several dances of complete bliss Lawrence asked her, "Hey would it be all right with you if I asked Melody to dance?"

Holland tried not to show her heart instantly sinking. "Sure." She smiled and went and sat down against the wall, wondering who else in the gym would ask her to dance, or who she could even stand next to and make small talk.

Holland didn't want to, didn't want to with every inch of herself, but she could not help watching Lawrence and Melody. Could not help noticing what a beautiful boy and girl they were. She watched them dancing, looking at each other, talking a little too intense. Holland wanted to look away, but stared any-way at the beautiful boy and the beautiful girl, who obviously had some kind of history.

After about one thousand years, the song finally end-ed. A very handsome native boy, who Holland supposed was Troy, swooped in and took Melody away from Lawrence.

Holland watched it thinking, if the boy had one brain in his head he would have seen Melody's disappointment and even anger when he broke in. But the handsome boy, Troy, must not have had even one brain in his head, because he was just smiling and acting like Melody was the lucky one, to be dancing with him.

Lawrence came back to her side. She spoke before she thought, "She is so beautiful. I wish I had some great looking guy giving you some competition. I read once that guys like girls more if that is going on."

She said it so straight forward, and as soon as the words were out of her mouth she nearly gasped in embarrassment. Her face glowed with warmth that she knew could only be red, red, red.

Lawrence started to laugh. He laughed hard and acted so entertained at her moroseness and embarrassment, that she started laughing also.

The next instant, making Holland's laugh freeze on her face, Melody stood at her side looking at her in disdain. "You've never introduced me to your friend," Melody said flatly.

Holland could not miss the second of annoyance that passed over Lawrence's face as he looked at Melody. But he immediately brought it under control, "Melody, this is Holland Adams. Holland, Melody Begaye."

"Why did you come to Holbrook?" Melody asked evenly, menacingly.

Holland felt her knees go weak. She took Lawrence's

arm to steady herself. "My dad, my dad got a job here." She hoped she didn't sound completely wimpy.

"When will the job be over?" Melody stepped in closer.

"I, I don't know," Holland felt the familiar anger surge through her.

Lawrence stepped between them. "Come on Melody, why?"

Melody looked at Lawrence, hurt filling her eyes. "Why? Why do you think, Lawrence?"

Lawrence took Holland by the hand, and dragged her to the door. They walked towards her home. He held her hand tightly. Holland breathed deep. The night air felt cool and smelled of fall. She wanted to talk to him about it, ask about the history between them, but she couldn't.

Instead, they talked about future plans with education. They talked about Luke. They talked about classes at school. Holland was careful not to bring up her mom, and she knew that Lawrence wouldn't talk about whatever he had been so upset about Monday, or about the incident with Melody tonight.

At the front door, Lawrence turned to Holland, and smiled his beautiful smile. "Holland, like the country," was all he said.

Holland smiled, wishing once again in life, that she was clever in conversation. But the more she tried, the worse her tongue became tied, so she just smiled.

Lawrence put his hands around her waist, and pulled her into him. Holland's heart pounded, she noticed again, that he smelled really good up close.

"Holland, like the country, I think I like you quite a bit," Lawrence said softly.

"Lawrence, the Navajo, I know I really like you," Holland whispered.

Lawrence smiled, his eyebrow raising.

"That didn't really come out how I wanted it to," Holland blushed brightly, shaking her head, and wincing. Before she could stop herself, she cursed under her breath, "dammit." This only adding to her blushing and alarm. "I am so sorry. I usually don't swear, well, in front of people."

Holland stopped herself, closed her eyes in exasperation and shook her head slightly.

All the while Lawrence was laughing. He pulled her in again to him and said, "Holland," He kissed her on the lips, softly and tenderly.

Holland reached her arms up around his neck and kissed him back, praying it seemed like she knew what she was doing. Then she pulled away in surprise, and once again spoke before she thought. "Wow that was so wonderful. Even better than I imagined it would be."

"Oh so you have imagined it quite a bit?" Lawrence teased.

And before she could stop herself she again spoke, "Yes, quite a bit."

But she didn't wince or look alarmed. She was comfortable with it. Lawrence smiled at her, and hugged her tight, then walked away.

Chapter Twenty Two

When Troy pulled Melody away from Lawrence at the dance, completely oblivious to her reaction, Melody wanted to pull his ear off.

She looked at him and rolled her eyes, hoping he would catch on to her annoyance, but no, of course not.

She looked over at Lawrence and Holland, both lit talking and laughing again. It was more than she could take. Without thinking she walked over to them.

She felt ashamed of herself when she questioned the girl. She knew Lawrence would be disgusted, but she couldn't stop herself. With the first question the girl looked like she would keel over. But with the second question, Melody saw a little fire light up in her eyes. She knew that fire. She knew what it meant. She begrudged it, but had to give the girl credit. She carried some fire.

As soon as Lawrence and the girl left, Troy once again was at her side.

"So you decided you are going to the Badlands with me after the dance?" He asked in his over eager way.

Melody studied him. Nothing about him could over-come the growing contempt she felt for him.

She didn't answer, didn't even reply. She danced with him, looking at anyone but him, but couldn't stop thinking about the way Lawrence had grabbed the girl's hand and left the dance. She looked at Troy's handsome face smiling at her, al-ways so pleased with himself.

"Okay," she said.

"Great!" Troy boomed back.

Melody cringed inside, feeling disgust for herself. Grateful her mom was coming to Holbrook in the morning to pick her up, so she wouldn't have to worry about that. The rest of the dance she tried not to think about her decision.

The Badlands were several miles out of Holbrook. It

was an area of sand dunes, washes and hills, dotted with a few sage bushes and cedar trees. Melody had heard several stories of mysterious events happening there that dated back to when her people were the only ones there.

After she changed out of her dress, and into jeans and a warm jacket, she went to the back of the dorm. Troy was in a borrowed car. He said it belonged to his cousin, who lived in Holbrook. No one else was in the car. She climbed in, feeling unsure.

Troy talked incessantly, about the game, about his greatness, about things she really didn't know about, because she tried hard not to listen. He didn't even need feedback; he just kept on talking.

Driving to the Badlands, it suddenly hit Melody that she was tired. Troy's never ending chatter, and the swaying car, feeling like a rocking chair, made it so Melody could barely keep her eyes open. It had been such a long, thoroughly miserable day. She worked hard not to think about the incident with Lawrence and the girl.

But the memory of them all lit up, and smiling at each other kept coming back, making her determined to stick with her decision.

Melody awoke with a start. She couldn't believe in the short drive she had fallen asleep. The car stopped and she felt Troy's arm around her. He had pulled her in close. She did not know why, but she felt so uncomfortable that she acted like she was still asleep.

Troy put the car into park with his left hand and turned the car off. She could hear kids gathering wood for a bon fire. Troy kept his arm around her with a tight grip on her shoulder.

Troy leaned towards her face. Melody could feel his breath on her. Her heart pounded. Suddenly, she felt his lips on hers, smashing, pushing, suffocating. She instantly stiffened, and with one move shoved Troy away and slid over to the pas-senger door.

As soon as she scrambled out of the car, before she got the door closed, Troy was there, trying to take her hand.

"You really are that clueless!" Melody said coldly.

"What?" asked Troy, a little too pleased with himself.

Melody walked over to the fire. Her pounding heart in-tensified. She could tell Troy liked her a lot. It did feel exciting to have the most popular boy in the school liking her. She could feel tonight the intensity of his emotions, and she had to admit; it felt good having him give her so much attention.

But Melody could not dismiss the kiss. It had felt horrible. And she could not push back the thought of Troy himself, so unappealing. She thought of the tender kiss, with Lawrence, when they discovered his mom's cancer.

Someone poured gas on the small fire. Quickly, it roared to a bonfire. It lit up the area and put off warmth immediately. Melody found a rock to sit on. She sat looking into the flames, trying to compose her feelings. Troy sat down beside her and again tried to take her hand.

"Hey back off a little," she told him.

"What, why? What am I doing?" he asked, acting innocent.

"Just because other girls seem to like you doing this, doesn't mean I do."

"I know," Troy said laughing. "I love a fight. I want to win."

"What?" Her excitement grew in time with her anger-- which only made her angrier. "So I am just some kind of game that you're trying to win?"

"No, no it's not like that," he soothed. "You're just not like all the other girls."

"If you knew what a stupid line that was, you would be embarrassed for yourself."

Troy seemed embarrassed and a little angry, Melody could see that he was not used to a girl not falling for his lines, but he smiled, "Let's just talk."

"Well, what did you think we would do?" she snorted, angry remembering that he had kissed her when he thought she was asleep.

"Come on, you know what we come out here for," Troy practically snarled back, his mood changing in an instant.

"No, I really don't," Melody matched his snarl. "You told me we were going to have a bonfire. I thought we would sit around it and talk!"

Melody looked around. Several kids were watching them. The bonfire blazed brightly. She had known in the back of her mind what the possibilities of coming here were. She had not allowed herself to think it through all the way. She had only reacted to seeing Lawrence with Holland. She needed to play it through coolly.

"So I bet it was a lot of fun playing that game tonight?" she asked brightly, her voice sounded fake.

Immediately Troy fell for the bait. "Oh man, that was the best, winning in the last minute. Those Tuba City guys thought they had us from the word go. They were so shocked to get beat like that!"

Melody could hardly remember the game. She realized she only watched Lawrence and Holland. "Tell me about your family," Melody continued.

"Well, I live in Many Farms. I have two older brothers and two younger brothers."

"Wow, five boys," Melody tried to act interested.

Just then, Melody saw Cody walk up out of the darkness, seemingly shocked to see her there with Troy. Melody cringed, afraid he would tell Lawrence, but her relief at seeing him overcame that.

"Hey, Cody," Melody greeted him warmly.

"What are you doing here?" Cody asked.

"I heard you were coming, and I thought I better come keep an eye on you." She sounded fake, even to herself,

Cody laughed. "Yeah, right!"

"Yeah, that is right!" her smile became more authentic.

Troy watched the exchange, a glum look on his face. The group of students was growing and so was the size of the bonfire. Several came with cases of beer. Melody watched with worried eyes about what was unfolding.

After a few minutes, Cody sat on the other side of her, "Melody, do you want to go back?"

"Yes," she tried not to act as worried as she felt.

"What? You've got to be kidding," Troy bellowed, roughly grabbing Melody's arm.

Before she could blink, Cody reached across her, snatching Troy's shirt. Melody leaned back as far as she could. Troy barked, "Let go of me."

"I'll be glad to, as soon as you leave," Cody answered calmly.

Cody stood and pulled Troy up with him. "Who do you think you are?" Troy's anger made his voice shake.

"Who do I think I am? No one really. Just a bull rider who knows how to treat a lady," Cody replied.

Troy opened his mouth to say something, but thought better of it, and stomped off.

Cody turned to Melody, pulling her up, "Come on, I'll take you back."

They walked to a pickup. Cody opened the door for her, walked around and got in. Melody was filled with gratitude, "It was really stupid of me to come. I should have known how it would be."

"Yeah, you are right," he seemed somewhat disbelieving. "Why did you do it?"

"You don't even want to know," she replied miserably.

"Yes, I do."

"Did you know I grew up next door to Lawrence?" Melody asked hesitantly.

"Yeah, so I've heard," Cody sighed.

"Well, I lived next to him until sixth grade. But I really care about him, I . . . I really love him."

"Lucky guy," Cody said without guile.

"Well, I don't think that's how he looks at it." Melody smiled sadly. "He has his little Holland girl."

"Yeah, he talks about her all the time," Cody laughed. "Maybe you should go for his roommate."

"Does he really, talk about her all the time?" Melody

blurted.

Cody sighed again, "Actually no. Well I've heard him talk about her, but I've also heard him talk about you. And you have to remember, guys are not like girls, sitting around talking about love and all."

"Please don't go tell Lawrence any of this," Melody shivered with embarrassment.

"I'll just tell him about the part about you loving him," Cody teased "The rest is a complete secret."

Melody slugged Cody in the arm, "Not a word, Cody! Anyways, he already knows it. I'm sure he doesn't want the school to know too."

"He knows you love him? What kind of idiot knows you love him and does nothing about it? I thought he was like all smart and everything," Cody said in amazement.

Melody felt an upwelling of warmth for Cody. He was so nice to talk to. He just said what he thought, didn't have to put everything in code.

"Why did your aunt and uncle raise you until the sixth grade?" he asked.

"My mom—my mom is an alcoholic," Melody revealed

apprehensively, "The tribe gave them custody of me at four months. But my mom is trying so hard now. She really is a good person."

"I'm sure she is," Cody said, again without guile, "So how does Lawrence know you love him?"

"Well, I only told him once and that was when my mom came to take me back to live with her in sixth grade. But Lawrence told me once that when things are important, you just kind of know without being told. Trouble is he may not think this is all that important," Melody sighed.

"Wow, he really is not all that smart," Cody responded.

"If I could ever just prove to him that I have changed. I used to always be in so much trouble," Melody grimaced, knowing the trouble was still there, just not in such big doses.

"I think I will have to clue him in," Cody said.

"No, no! Promise me you won't ever, ever say anything about this.

"He really is an idiot," Cody replied with wonder. He smiled, "Lawrence just doesn't know how to feel the right things."

Melody laughed. They pulled up a half block from the

dorm. "Walk quietly to the west side door," Cody explained, "It will be open, go straight to your room."

"Really, for sure?" she asked in a sudden panic.

"Yes, really for sure," Cody smiled. "There is only one dorm aide on tonight and we have connections with him."

"Connections?"

"What you don't know won't hurt you," Cody reached over her and opened her door. "Now off you go, and be quiet." Before he pulled away he looked at her, "You are beautiful Melody. You really are."

Her heart melted. "You are so nice Cody. That means more to me than you know."

He smiled almost sad like, "Hate the sound of that reply."

"Well you shouldn't. I love hearing you say that."

She got out of the truck and ran quietly to her room.

Chapter Twenty Three

"Holland? Holland are you awake?" Luke whispered.

She reluctantly opened one eye to look at him. He was sitting on the edge of her bed looking concerned.

"What?" Holland sleepily asked.

"Holland, I'm worried about Mom."

"What? Where's Dad?" Holland tried not to sound as cross as she felt.

"Dad went to work for a couple of hours."

It was Saturday morning, before the Thanksgiving break. Homecoming had been three sweet weeks before. Holland did not want to wake up and think about the mess at home.

She sat up, rubbing her eyes, the light hurting them,

"What are you worried about Luke?"

"Mom is in her room and she is making a lot of noise."

"What kind of noise?"

"Like banging around noise, like she is moving furniture or something."

Holland climbed out of bed. She didn't need the bother. It would just be a conglomerated mess. No, that was not the word because conglomerate meant to merge. Holland wondered how the heck she could ever merge with her mom, or even her dad. Luke, she thought, she and Luke could conglomerate just fine. But she and her mother would be like oil and water trying to mix. Shake the jar really hard and they seemed to conglomerate, but in a few short seconds, they'd repel one another.

Holland dragged over to her mother's bedroom door and stood and listened. Luke stood behind her. He was right. There was a whole lot of noise coming from the room. Holland knocked softly. There was no answer. She knocked harder, getting angry.

Holland opened the door. Their mother was standing, fully dressed, pushing her dresser across the floor.

"What are you doing?" Holland asked, rolling her eyes.

"I'm rearranging my room, cleaning it up. It's a complete mess!" Mom answered in a voice Holland and Luke had not heard in a long while. The room was a complete mess. Those days even Dad did not use it as his room, but slept on the couch, and kept his clothes in the laundry room.

Holland and Luke looked at each other, Luke smiling, Holland feeling put out. She shook her head annoyed at Luke's happy reaction. Luke went in to help. She wasn't about to feel hope over it and walked back to her room, crawling in bed. She had seen these mood swings before with her mother.

Holland lay in bed thinking about Thanksgiving break. They had Wednesday, Thursday, and Friday off. Dad had the time off work. Holland had wondered if her mother would have time off from her bedroom, maybe this was the answer.

Holland hated to wonder anything about her mother. She knew that the anger, she was fighting off so well, could jump out from behind the curtains. She angered at finding no answers, no understanding, no nothing, just reckless, writhing emotion, with nothing to learn from it but how terrible it felt. That was the only information that ever came, was just how completely engulfing and horrible it all felt, nothing to learn from it but to avoid it at all costs.

Holland forced her mind away from it. She thought about Lawrence, and gradually fell back asleep.

# # #

Dad shook her gently. He quietly told her to get dressed, that they were going to go shopping for Thanksgiving dinner. Holland said she would go get Luke. Dad shook his head and said no, that he was still helping Mom clean her room. He seemed happy about it.

The morning was chilly and their breath showed in the air. In the car, Dad blasted the heater, but did not drive straight to the store. Holland looked at him, saying nothing. Finally, across town, by the covered and locked up swimming pool he spoke.

"Holland, how is it going for you here?"

The anger, that Holland had stifled from a few hours earlier, quickly boiled to the top. "Well Dad, we moved to another state, another world really. Mom stays locked in her bedroom, but this morning, she is awake and cleaning. I'm worried about Luke, but he is probably doing better than me."

Holland felt all the more angry, when tears escaped and rolled down her cheeks. She turned away from him staring out the window at the desolate town. "Is that the best you can do? Asking me how is it going here?"

In disbelief her mind thought of Lawrence. He and Luke were absolutely the only reason she found hope in living in Holbrook. She wondered if Lawrence really knew about her life, if he would ever want anything to do with her again,

Holland wished her dad had not asked that stupid question. She only wanted to skate the surface of the water. A stupid question like that plunged her into a deep dive.

Holland could not speak. She sat looking out the window trying to blink back tears and not look too pitiful. She must not have pulled that off. She must have looked completely pitiful, because in response her dad looked completely pitiful himself. He took her hand and neither spoke.

He drove to the grocery store parking lot. He parked using one hand, his other hand held Holland's so tightly she wanted to wince. She knew it was Dad's way of letting her know he cared. But she still felt anger.

After a long while, with Dad holding her hand, and the

heater blasting, heat and warmth filled every little nook and corner of the car. As Holland let the warmth engulf her body, she felt comfortable, nervous about the weekend and Mother, but peaceful.

After shopping, they drove home. As they unloaded the car, Luke came outside, his face pale showing concern.

"Dad," he said worriedly, then looked at Holland and seemed to stop himself.

"What, Luke?" Holland asked, exasperated that he felt the need to be careful talking around her.

"Dad," Luke continued, but with his eyes on her, "I think you should be in the bedroom with Mom. I was just trying to help her clean up her room, and now she is, she's . . ."

Dad grabbed another grocery bag and walked into the house. Holland and Luke followed through the kitchen, then down the hall. He knocked on the door. "Annie," he said quietly as he opened the door. Behind him Holland could see her mother standing on the bed, reaching towards the ceiling, trying to undo the light fixture over the bed.

"Annie," Dad said again as he stepped to the bed. "What are you doing? Let me help you down."

"No!" Mother yelled, half laughing, and half angry, "I hate this light. I've looked at it for months. It has to be the ugliest thing I've ever laid eyes on. I can't believe you let me lay here just looking at this ugly light. You should have been the one to change it!"

With that, her mother jumped up and smashed the glass light fixture with her fist. It crashed down on the bed and the floor in pieces. Holland and Luke jumped back. Dad charged in and grabbed her mother, trying to wrestle her away from the broken glass on the bed.

She was screaming, crying, laughing. Luke and Holland stood frozen watching.

"Annie, stop. Annie, please stop, not in front of the kids, please."

"Mother!" Holland exploded, "Stop! Get a hold of yourself!"

The room went quiet. She stopped her laughing and crying combination and looked over at Holland with a curious look.

"What?" she asked.

"You could make the choice not to do this. Get control

of yourself and don't do this!" Holland's voice sounded less an-gry and more desperate.

"Is that what you think?" Her mother asked, sounding like she was all there.

"You don't have to freak out. You just don't," Holland's voice became very quiet.

Her mother stood leaning heavily into Dad, considering the words intently. The air in the room felt heavy, and Holland struggled to catch her breath.

"I guess . . . I guess, that's right. I guess I am deciding to do this. I guess it is choice and I guess that makes me very bad," she said it so sincerely, not as if she was trying to be a martyr.

Holland watched the energy drain right out of her mother and on the floor with the broken glass. It was as tangi-ble as anything she ever witnessed. It returned her mother to her usual self, limp, sad, and teary-eyed. Holland felt dreadful remorse, like she'd pulled the plug. Dad and Luke tried to not act like she had been the one, but she felt sure that in their hearts that was what they felt. It was her fault.

Chapter Twenty Four

That morning before school, Lawrence sat on his bed,
packing his bag for the game. Basketball season had started
and that made time feel even more crunched. He was a starter
on the boys' freshmen team. Melody made the starting five of
the Junior Varsity team, which was even more of an achieve-
ment. He would never admit it but he felt secretly glad. The J.V.
games were played before the freshman games. Lawrence
often got the chance to watch Melody play.

It was close to Christmas and the last day of school
before the two-week Christmas break. Later that afternoon
Holbrook was playing basketball in Winslow.

Before school that morning, while packing, Lawrence
relived the moment when his dad finally told him the truth.

His dad had grown emotional telling Lawrence about it.

Something Lawrence rarely saw. Antonia was scheduled to start chemotherapy after Christmas.

Henry firmly stated that Lawrence would wait until his mother chose to talk to him about it, that he should wait for her.

"But she must have figured out I know!" Lawrence had erupted.

"I don't really know," Henry said wistfully, "if she does or not."

Lawrence felt frustrated but understood. Neither of his parents had ever been very talkative. It seemed as if they communicated silently. Lawrence always respected the silence. He always felt he could understand what they communicated silently.

That was, until recently. When he went to Holbrook during the school week, he felt out of the loop on weekends when he returned. His mother still adored him and gave him attention when he was home, but her mind seemed far away.

Lawrence knew his mother was strong, would always be strong. It was just her way of dealing with it. He needed to try and respect that.

Lawrence finished packing his bag and walked to the

high school. He felt excited that his parents would be in Winslow to attend his game, and then he would ride home with them for Christmas break. He hoped and prayed that his mom would talk to him over Christmas, that somehow she could tell him everything, and that she could reassure him that she would be okay.

Riding on the bus to Winslow he sat two seats behind Melody. Of course Troy, who started on the varsity basketball team, crowded in next to her. It angered Lawrence, watching Troy touch Melody a million times. He touched her hair, her shoulder, her arm, even her face. Constantly smiling and laughing like he was all that and a bag of chips.

Cody had accidentally let it slip to Lawrence that Melody had gone to the bon-fire party after Homecoming. Cody caught himself after it was out and guardedly told him how upset Melody became at the sight of the beer and that he took her back to the dorm.

Lawrence sneered at this explanation, and felt shocked when Cody grabbed his arm roughly, "You are so stupid Lawrence. Why do you question if I am telling you the truth? Have I ever lied to you?"

"Well, no," Lawrence answered, shocked by Cody's intense reaction.

"Then don't question me now. That is exactly what happened," Cody exploded.

Suddenly Lawrence felt just as angry, "Well what in the heck was she doing there in the first place?"

"Cut her some slack. She is as dumb as you!" And with that Cody got up to leave the room, stopping at the door to add, "And just so you know up front, I like her too. So hopefully she won't stay dumb about you for long!" With that he walked out with a slam.

Troy's loud laugh brought Lawrence's thoughts back to the bus. He watched the backs of Melody and Troy's heads. At least, he thought with some satisfaction, Melody didn't gush over him like all the other girls in school. In fact, she always treated him rather coolly. But that seemed to only make Troy like her more.

Lawrence's thoughts jumbled through his head. He thought of the day when he and Melody figured out about his mother's cancer. He had felt so close to her and appreciative of her comfort. But back at school that Monday, without planning to, he asked Holland to the Homecoming game the first moment he saw her.

When he thought about it, he'd immediately had broken off the closeness he felt with Melody. He did a pretty good job at it. Melody acted hurt for a week or two, and then angry and cold. They had barely even spoken since that fall day.

Lawrence thought about how often he talked with Holland and enjoyed it. But he felt forced to acknowledge something he had not been willing to before. He looked forward to watching Melody play basketball, more than even his own games, and he loved basketball. He remembered the kiss with Melody before school started; he remembered kissing Holland after homecoming. His mind swirled.

Suddenly, shocking Lawrence, and making his heart jump into his throat, Melody stood and walked back to his seat. She sat next to him. Lawrence ignored Troy who turned and stared.

"Uh, hi," Lawrence said nervously.

"I just wanted to tell you that we are spending Christmas with Auntie Red and Uncle Tilden," she said quietly and coldly.

"Oh!" The news surprised him.

Melody shed her coldness. "Lawrence, how is your mom?"

Lawrence hesitated before answering, "My dad finally told me over Thanksgiving. But my mother still won't talk to me about it. She starts treatments after Christmas."

"It must be hard, being around her and not being about to ask about it."

"It's strange. I can tell she's preoccupied with things. She acts like I don't notice anything, but she must know," he'd started speaking fast and when he realized it he cut himself off, almost embarrassed.

Melody was looking down at her hands. They both became silent.

In the gym, Nascha, Auntie Red, Uncle Tilden, Sage, Tilden Jr. and even his grandma and grandpa were there. Lawrence could watch the first half of Melody's game, and then he needed to go dress out for his.

Everyone seemed happy, with Christmas break beginning. Lawrence noticed even his mom and dad seemed light-hearted.

Lawrence's eyes felt stuck to Melody as he watched her warm up for her game. Troy and a few of his friends also sat watching.

Sticky like glue, Lawrence thought disgustedly.

The game started. The tip-off went straight to her, Melody's hands were shaking and she lost hold of the ball. Lawrence saw Melody clench her teeth. He could visibly see the hot surge of familiar anger flowing. She breathed deeply, calmed herself, and focused on the game.

Melody glanced up at Lawrence and gave him a look that seemed to say, "Who cares about stupid Lawrence, and his stupid crush on that stupid Holland?" Lawrence could not help but smile.

After the first quarter, his dad, sitting next to him, leaned over. "She is a beautiful player."

Lawrence thought about the statement and wondered if he meant she was a beautiful girl that plays basketball, or a girl that played basketball beautifully. Lawrence said nothing in re-ply but decided Melody was both. Reluctantly at halftime, Lawrence pulled himself away to dress out for his own game.

Chapter Twenty Five

Lawrence didn't know that after her game Melody, showered and dressed as quickly as possible to get back into the gym for Lawrence's game. The varsity boys played at the same time in another gym and he knew that Troy must have repeatedly asked Melody to watch his game.

The first quarter was half way through. Lawrence glanced at Melody as soon as she sat down by her mother.

Lawrence struggled to tune Melody out, frustrated that once again he let her affect him this way, affect him at all. But he could not stop himself from glancing up to see her, wondering if she would stay or go into the larger gym and watch Troy's game.

Lawrence felt further frustrated because his game did

not go well. He did not play to his potential and felt continually distracted. A few times he could hear his family yelling for him, encouraging him. He got hung up on the fact that with every-one watching, he was playing poorly. His team lost.

After the game Lawrence hurried into the locker rooms to avoid talking to anyone. He showered slower than he should have, making everyone wait. When he finally emerged from the locker room, everyone was standing around, even Grandma and Grandpa.

Grandpa put his arm around Lawrence, "Good game son."

Lawrence grimaced, humilliated because he knew they knew darn well that it had not been a good game. He glanced over at Melody, then marched towards the door, leaving his family to follow. Embarrassed by his actions he waited at the front door of the gym and forced a smile.

"Aw come on Lawrence," Uncle Tilden said laughing, "You didn't play that terrible, just a little like a white boy!"

The whole family erupted into titters and giggles, wait-ing for Lawrence's reaction.

Lawrence's anger and embarrassment spilled out, "I

don't think I played as bad as a white boy, just more like a girl."

There was a shameful pause from everyone and finally his dad said quietly, "No, Lawrence, if you had played like Melody tonight, your team would have won."

Lawrence's face flushed a deep red, and Uncle Tilden put his arm around Lawrence's shoulder, "Lawrence we know you are not a white boy. It is very clear right now you are a red man."

Lawrence could not help himself and laughed, ashamed of his words. He glanced again at Melody but she ignored him. The entire group went to a cafe to eat a late supper. Lawrence, still embarrassed at his rudeness, and still a little angry at playing that badly, tried not to, but found himself sitting next to Melody.

"Good game," he said lamely.

Melody turned with disgust, fire in her eyes, and did not reply.

Lawrence tried again, "How many points did you have?"

Melody shook her head, her eyes burning with loathing.

"I think you had like eight points at the half when I left to get dressed out," he added meekly.

"Don't."

"Don't what?" Lawrence asked, trying to act innocently friendly.

"Don't say something like you said in the gym and try to act like it was nothing."

Lawrence sat next to Melody, neither saying anything, feeling like lumps on a log. They ate their hamburgers in silence while the family talked and joked.

Lawrence sat watching his family. Everyone was in a light-hearted, happy mood, laughing and teasing. Finally, the meal ended and Lawrence rode with his parents and Melody with her mom.

His mind churned with agitation. She frustrated him way down inside. He thought about kissing her in the wash. He thought about how good she looked playing basketball. He thought about her almost fighting in the cafeteria with Toshee. He thought about Troy pawing her. He thought about her until they got home.

Chapter Twenty Six

As the last day of school ended, before the Christmas break began, Holland could not help but feel dread. Of course she looked forward to spending more time with Luke. He was her best friend, one of her only friends. But as she walked out of the school and into the cold, she could not help but to feel that the family felt more disjointed than ever.

Holland found Luke standing in the cold, on the corner of the high school, waiting for her. She wondered if he did that because he did not want to go home alone. She didn't blame him if that was the reason.

They walked in silence. Holland couldn't believe the first semester of her 9th grade was over. She thought about Lawrence, and then Melody. She felt worry and dread every time she was in Melody's presence. Holland thought if looks could kill she would definitely be dead, even though Melody had spoken barely five words to her.

"We made it through the first half of the school year," Luke broke through her thoughts.

"Yeah, we sure did."

"You like Lawrence don't you."

Holland turned to smile at Luke, "Yeah, I'd be lying if I said I don't. I like him . . ."

Luke smiled broadly. And before she could stop herself she added, "There is a girl named Melody. She likes him too. I think they sort of grew up together."

"No one could compete with you Holland."

Holland put her arm around Luke's shoulder, "At least I have your vote. But don't you ever feel that it is a whole different world here, a culture, traditions, that are completely foreign. There is like this whole Navajo culture that Lawrence and Melody have together, that I'm not a part of."

"Yeah, but they're not that different. I think the kids in my class . . . I think we are a lot alike," Luke replied simply.

"He cares about doing well in school. He's probably the

only ninth grader ahead of me."

"See, he's a lot like you," Luke beamed.

"He is. I mean I can talk to him easier than I've ever talked to any guy. But sometimes I learn things about Navajos and it feels really different."

Holland shivered, wondering if Lawrence felt and saw differences with her and he didn't even know the biggest parts of her life.

"Hey," Luke said, interrupting her deep thoughts.

"Hey you," Holland replied smiling.

"I think it's really interesting here," he said.

"I think I agree."

Then Holland felt once again engulfed in her thoughts. She was starting to learn about the Navajo culture, learn about their traditions. She was beginning to understand that Navajo way of life seemed everything to Lawrence. It was what he was, his very existence.

Holland looked at Luke, "I wonder how different Navajos are today than they were in the Old West."

Luke was immediately drawn in, "Well, they probably look the same. But they didn't speak English. We are reading this book in class, <u>Sing Down The Moon</u>, about their forced march from Canyon de Chelly. The government forced all the Navajos to walk to Fort Sumner in New Mexico. It was like hundreds of miles and a ton of the tribe died. The Navajos called it the Long Walk. I can't believe people thought it was okay to do something like that."

Holland listened, agreeing with Luke's answer to her question. He continued, excited to share his knowledge, "And later, they started forcing Navajo kids to go into government schools. They changed their names from Navajo to English. They cut their hair. They whipped them if they spoke Navajo. They took them from their families."

"Sounds horrible," Holland said, surprised at his knowledge of Navajo history, way more than she knew. "It makes you wonder what we are doing today that in a hundred or so years, they will say; wonder why they let people do that?"

Luke stopped in his tracks, grabbing Holland's arm, his voice choking back sudden tears. "I've already been thinking about that Holland. I think the thing in a hundred years that people will wonder about is . . . why didn't we help people like mom?"

Holland's eyes burned with tears. Luke was such a better person than she was. Instead of the anger and annoyance toward their mother, he wanted to help her.

She hugged him, "I think you hit it right on the nose Luke, right on the nose."

They walked on in silence. It was too painful for Holland to think about her mother. She let her mind go back to Lawrence.

Holland knew that the Navajo culture was evolving. She could see that by all the differences of Navajo students in school. The culture was as diverse as the number of Navajos belonging to it. Holland wondered if Lawrence saw that.

Luke interrupted Holland's thoughts, "Holland, my friend, Cordell, told me that the guy who drove into the train was controlled by a skinwalker. Have you heard of those?" his voice was quiet and worried.

"A what?"

"A skinwalker," Luke continued, "they are like witches that can take the form of animals and make their victims hurt themselves and others."

"Do you believe in that kind of stuff?" Holland looked at

Luke matter of fact as they entered their yard.

"I don't know. I think there is a lot of stuff out there we don't know about. Cordell sure believes in them." Luke looked at her with big eyes.

She shrugged, "Sounds like a lot of superstitious rubbish."

Sometimes, walking home from school, dread flooded Holland. Since Thanksgiving, their mother stayed even more in her room. Holland figured she had to come out during the day once in a while, because when the family was home, their mother stayed in her room. Their dad mostly quit trying to go in, because most days he was locked out.

She sometimes wondered if her mother was even alive in her room. What the heck was going on in there?

As they entered the house, their mother was sitting on the sofa in her bathrobe. Luke was immediately at her side next to the sofa, hugging her. She knew better than to ask Holland to sit next to her.

Holland felt immediate disgust watching Luke, like a wind-up toy, going full force, trying not to run out of juice. He knew, when he let the conversation lag just a little, the wet blanket would fall back on their mother.

"How are you feeling?" he asked their mother.

She glanced at Holland hesitating. "I'm okay . . . doing okay."

Holland felt her eyes involuntarily roll back. It was so painful to watch.

"School is going really well. I really like it here!" Luke was so eager.

"Oh Luke, that makes me happy, really happy." Their mother smiled, her eyes shining under the dark circles.

Holland had to wonder if her mother had ever experienced a happy moment in her life, the way she looked just then.

"Here are my grades!" Luke pulled a wadded up paper from his pocket. "I got most A's, a few B's. But I'm sure Holland got straight A's as usual!" Luke beamed at Holland.

"Yeah, which you would have known if you had gone to parent teacher conference." It was out before she thought it through. But then the anger pushed her on. "I bet you don't even know the classes I'm taking, do you?"

Luke hung his head, and Holland watched her mother's

eyes go from shining to looking dull. Hopeless and dull. Holland immediately regretted her words, but the anger hung over her, like dense fog.

Holland closed her eyes, and saw the man from the train wreck smiling at her, laughing happily at her. Quickly she opened her eyes, wanting to make it better.

"I mean, if you just came out of your room more, you'd know so much more about everything," The look on her mother's face let her know it hadn't helped much.

"Do do you like it here?" Her mother's directness shocked Holland.

Several images passed through her mind, the man at the train wreck, Lawrence, Melody, Luke, her dad. "I'm trying to make it work," was all she could think to say.

Her mother stood up and walked to Holland. She touched Holland's face gently. "I'm glad you're trying," she said softly and kissed Holland on the forehead, and walked back to her bedroom closing the door.

Holland blinked back tears. "Convoluted. Strange. Crazy," she said feeling, strangely enough, a little happy.

Luke still wiping tears from his eyes, grinned, "Holland,

sometimes you are thinking so hard that you start saying what you think out loud."

"Well that's exactly what it is Luke, convoluted, strange, crazy. I don't know what to think, most times I just try not. Sometimes don't you just want to scream at Dad and ask him why the heck he does not do something about Mom?"

Luke considered that for a moment and Holland went on. "When we were smaller, he constantly tried to do things about it. Now it seems like he has shut down from trying."

"Maybe we should do something about it," he said half worried about Holland's reaction and half hopeful.

Holland gulped back a rush of emotion. Her reaction to Mom's situation was always anger and disgust. Luke's was always kindness. Holland tried not to let the thoughts that always nipped at the edge of her mind, the worried thoughts about when she graduated from high school, when she went to college. She wondered how she could ever leave Luke alone in all the convoluted, strange and crazy.

"What could we do?" she asked wearily.

"I don't know. But we are a family and we love each other," he simply said.

Holland hugged Luke tight, partly because she loved him, and partly to avoid having him see the tears that burned her eyes. "I know one thing we could do before Dad gets home. Let's get this place looking like Christmas is almost here. And then let's make some supper!"

Luke smiled happily. Holland smiled, but grimaced inside, wondering how she could teach Luke not to be nice, to try and take care of himself a little. He would get eaten alive by life. She had a sinking feeling, knowing that it would be about as possible as teaching her how to be nice.

"Hey, do you think you will see Lawrence over Christmas break?" Luke asked in a teasing voice.

Holland knew Lawrence was playing basketball in Winslow. She had wanted in the worst way to go on the rooter bus and watch. But she knew Dad would not be home from work and she wouldn't leave Luke at home alone with Mother.

They put on Christmas music. Holland turned it up loud, knowing Mother could never sleep through it. They decorated the house with every decoration from the Christmas boxes they could find. They made some delicious tostadas, and popped the cork on a bottle of root beer.

Sitting with Luke, eating, a strange thing happened. Holland suddenly felt sweet, happy, and peaceful. She looked at Luke and felt a surge of love for him that she could not describe. The feeling was so strong that Holland knew she would always hold the memory close.

"Do you think if we still lived in California, we would be experiencing there, what we are here, right this very minute? I mean how would our mother be doing there? How would we be doing there?" She asked Luke.

Luke looked at her quizzically. "Huh?"

"Do you think we are meant to be here?"

"Kind-of . . . Yeah."

Chapter Twenty Seven

For the entire weekend before Christmas, Melody
stayed busy and avoided Lawrence. She wrapped presents for
Auntie Red and played card games with Tilden Jr. and Gogo.
Monday was Christmas Eve.

Melody awoke to a dark, overcast day with snow blan-
keting. She lay in bed snuggled in the warmth of her covers
enjoying the quiet of the snow and everyone still asleep. Her
mind drifted to Lawrence. She had seen him chopping wood
and doing chores for his parents and grandparents, but he
somehow managed to avoid her as well as she avoided him.

She lay staring out of the window wondering why he
was such an idiot boy sometimes. She nearly jumped out of her

skin when his face popped up outside the window. He smiled broadly and motioned for her to join him.

He did not wait for her so after she pulled a coat and boots over her pajamas, she walked down to find him sitting on the large, old log. The cedar trees and sagebrush were weighted with snow, the rocky hills surrounding the wash, usually painted in purple and gold had become a blinding white.

Lawrence watched her with a fixed stare. She walked to him and he brushed snow off the log so she could sit. Lawrence reached over and took Melody's hand it shocked her. After several moments he turned to her and said, "I know I am a dumb jerk."

A laugh burst from her, "You can say that again!"

"I know I am dumb jerk," he said again. "You played so good. It flat out made me jealous," he added quietly.

She gave him a bewildered look, "We don't play against each other. Why do you compete with me?"

They sat in silence as the snowflakes grew heavier, the feeling of the storm settling in. Finally, Lawrence shook his head and said, "I don't really know why I feel competitive with you. I guess I just do that pretty much all the time."

"You feel like you are competing with me in school?" Melody asked, surprised.

"I feel like I am competing with everyone, well, maybe not Cody," he added half laughing. He immediately grew serious again, "I don't know why I do that. It is really stupid and I am supposed to be smart."

"It just doesn't make sense to me. You are the smartest kid in the school. You don't have to compete. You just have that already."

Lawrence looked at her long and hard, "I guess I know that in school, but not in sports and not with friends."

"But you are good in basketball and everyone tries to be your friend. I just don't get it," Melody examined him.

"Everyone? Why don't you?" Lawrence burst in defensively.

"You question my friendship?"

He answered softly, "Yeah, I guess I do. I mean no, I don't."

"I can't believe that!" Melody exploded. "I cannot believe that you even wonder about that. How could I make it more obvious?" Melody added angrily.

"Well, Troy is after you. Cody wants to be after you."

"And just what the heck to you mean by that? Is this part of that competition you were talking about? What about that stupid Holland girl?" Melody yelled.

Lawrence stood up with his back to her. Melody sat gasping in the cold air. "Hey, let's just calm down. It seems like we can hardly talk any more without getting angry," Lawrence said, as if he was trying to sound calm.

"Don't start telling me to calm down. I'll yell if I want to, and I feel like it," And with that she howled a loud coyote howl.

Lawrence started laughing and after a few seconds Melody joined in.

"You know what frustrates me Lawrence? I can't ever stay mad when I see your big white teeth."

Lawrence grabbed Melody's arm and pulled her gently up next to him, "Big white teeth huh?"

"Yeah, big white teeth, you don't have to compete with anyone over that one. You have the biggest, whitest teeth in the school," Melody grabbed Lawrence's arm and shook it back harder. "Why do you do that?" she asked.

"Show you my teeth?" Lawrence teased, showing his

teeth.

"No, doubt how I feel about you."

Lawrence looked her in the eyes. "I don't know Melody. I guess because I don't know for sure how I feel all the time, and I just assume you are in the same boat."

She blinked back tears, "You don't know how you feel?"

"Well, yes and no, sometimes I know exactly how I feel, but sometimes I just know. I know I don't want to feel what I feel."

The tears escaped and rolled down her face. "That does not make any sense."

"I know, I know, most of the time I can't even figure it out," he said softly.

Melody's tears continued harder and faster, and her nose started running. "Figure out what? This is not that hard."

"It is for me, Melody."

"What is?" she was yelling again, but couldn't help it, "either you care about me or you do not."

Lawrence looked like his own tears were about to fall, "Oh Melody never doubt that. I do care about you. It's just, that feels like the problem."

Melody, who had smiled softly when Lawrence said he cared about her, suddenly felt the cold of the snow that was covering her hat and coat. "Why is that a problem?" she asked numbly.

"Do you really want to hear this or know this?"

"Does this have something to do with being a traditional Navajo?" Melody spat out.

"No. Well, yes and no. It is just that . . ."

"What?" Melody pleaded.

"It is just that sometimes I am afraid of how I feel about you," Lawrence spoke so quietly that she wondered if she had heard him right.

She grew quiet. "I don't get it. I don't know what you mean. Why do keep saying sometimes? You either feel it or you don't."

One tear ran down Lawrence's cheek. He brushed it away, embarrassed. "It's just that once in a while I feel a feeling so strong towards you that I, I . . ."

"Oh, Lawrence, that is incredible. That makes me so happy."

Lawrence winced, "No, no Melody, don't be happy about what I am saying. It is not happy. I don't feel happy when I feel that feeling. It scares me. It is not good," he said firmly.

"Not good?" She was genuinely confused, "It sounded really good to me."

Lawrence smiled feebly, "I don't like how the feeling of, of how feeling so strong about you makes me feel. I don't want you to be able to control me like that."

The snow was falling heavily, weighing her down. She sat feeling like a small rabbit caught in a snare. With tears and snow on her face, her nose running, she said, "Lawrence I would never want to control you. I love you the way you are. I don't want to change you."

Lawrence looked like his heart was growing heavier and heavier, cold and heavy like the snow. "Melody I don't know if I can make you understand. I don't think you want to control me. I just feel like you could, not even trying."

Melody slowly stood, shaking the snow from her hat and coat, her sadness oozed through her every movement. "Maybe we should get back. They will wonder where we are."

"Melody, I am sorry I even told you that stuff. I only

wanted to apologize."

She started to walk away but turned back and with as much firmness as she could muster replied, "Lawrence, please don't apologize. I am glad you tried to explain to me how you feel. I can handle it. At least I am going to try."

They walked slowly out of the wash without another word.

Chapter Twenty Eight

Melody stripped her coat and hat off, untangled herself from her wet clothes, and put dry pajamas on, and crawled back into bed. Feeling cold and chilled inside and out, she lay shivering, the wet from her hair melting and running across her face. Her tears added to the wetness.

Finally, Nascha could take the pitiful scene no longer. She climbed into the small bed next to Melody. She put her arms around her and pulled her close. Melody, feeling the sympathy shown her, could not continue to cry as softly and sobs welled out from deep within her.

"Honey, what is it?" Nascha asked softly.

Melody could not answer for several moments. She rarely saw Melody cry, let alone so intensely. Eventually, her tears were cried out.

"I've just been down in the wash talking to Lawrence."

"And?"

"And he probably told me more about how he feels than ever in his life."

Nascha nodded.

With that a fresh wave of tears flowed down Melody's face. "I guess it is a good thing if I wanted to know how he really felt and not just some dream of how I hoped he felt. Mom, it feels like my insides are breaking. I love Lawrence as much as I love even you. I have loved him all my life and I think I always will."

Nascha looked shocked, "Melody you don't know how your feelings will be once you get out of high school. They will probably change three times between now and then."

I know I am young. And I am pretty sure this is how I will feel for all my life," she replied resolutely.

Nascha looked at her daughter and sighed, "You have always possessed a fierce independence and spirit, and quite likely do know your feelings. Melody I have always known you were an old spirit, a spirit far more mature than your physical body. I also know Lawrence, and understand why he inspires such intense feelings from you. Melody, I've always felt and saw that he cares about you also."

Melody felt surprised, but grateful her mom would talk so candid. "That's what I feel so confused about. He said he has strong feelings for me. Then he said it is not a happy thing for him to have, and that he does not want them," Melody replied, shivering miserably.

"Sweetie, maybe he recognizes it is because you are both too young to feel such serious feelings. Maybe it is a good thing," Nascha tried to sound hopeful.

"He said he doesn't want me to have control over him."

"Oh," answered Nascha, as if seeing it all much clearer, "well I think I can understand just a little where he may be coming from. It is dangerous to give somebody or something that much control over you."

"Mom you make it sound like I am bad for him! Like I am what alcohol is to you."

Nascha laughed softly. "Melody you probably made exactly the point he tried to make to you."

"That I get him drunk?" Melody replied, confused.

Nascha was still smiling, "Well in a way, yes."

She grew serious and sat up crossed legged next to Melody. "If you are old enough to have that conversation with Lawrence, you are old enough to hear me say this. Lawrence feels towards you the way a man feels towards a woman. Those are very intense feelings at times. Lawrence has a plan for his life. He is a very upright traditional young man. It probably frightens him to feel such intense feelings for a girl that he thinks can be trouble. Does that make sense to you?"

"You sound like I am a really bad girl. Doesn't anyone see how hard I have tried to change?" Melody moaned.

Everyone can clearly see how much better you are controlling your temper. But that is only a part of the issue. He feels strongly about you and doesn't know for sure, can't know for sure yet, if you should be part of his future plans."

Those words stung Melody unlike any she had ever heard. Coming from her mom, she finally understood what Lawrence had been trying to tell her. "I always thought if you loved someone you just made them part of your life and worked through things," she said haltingly.

Then Melody paused and grew angry, "He just wants

someone like Holland, some nice, perfect girl who will never have an opinion or never cross him on. He just wants a statue, not a real person. He says he cares so much about being traditional Navajo and she is not even Navajo!"

Melody's intensity was rising, "He just wants a pretend life. He just worries about how he comes across, not he what really is, or how he really feels! Lawrence is an idiot!"

Nascha shook her head half smiling and half frowning. Melody rolled to her side, away from her mother. Nascha sighed and climbed out of the bed and started to dress.

Melody lay breathing hard, feelings of frustration flowing through her veins. Every time she tried to think through the conversation her mind hit a brick wall and the frustration would swell up and flow out through her tears. Melody never cried so many tears in her entire life.

A few hours later, Melody awoke with a start. It was late in the morning. She jumped out of bed and quickly dressed, refusing to think about the events of a few hours earlier. She had only so much emotion within her and she felt that she already gave every inch of it and then some.

As Melody entered the kitchen, Auntie Red, Sage and

her mom were busy preparing food for the Christmas Eve feast. The mutton stew began to simmer on the stove. Melody breathed deeply nearly filling her mouth up on the smell alone. The wonderful aroma of thick chunks of mutton and loads of vegetables, all in a savory sauce, warmed up the kitchen as much as the snow put cold on the outside. Nascha put Melody to work kneading the dough for the fry bread.

The hot soapy dishwater steamed up the kitchen window. Melody wiped the window to look outside. With the work finished, she put on her coat and boots and told her mom she was going on a walk in the snow.

Leaving the house, Melody felt enthralled with the thick cover of snow that blanketed everything. Several more inches had fallen since that morning. Instead of the snow feeling heavy like it did earlier, Melody thought it felt more like a protective blanket falling over the world. It comforted her.

The cold burned up her nose and into her lungs when she breathed. As she walked, each step fell through the snow with a small crunch. Melody breathed deeply the bite of the air. Each breath seemed to cleanse her. With the crying and the cooking from before, the air and walk felt wonderful.

Suddenly welling up inside, she felt courage. Lawrence loved her. That was enough. Never mind that he was not always happy to do so. She felt she knew and understood something that he did not. That the pieces did not all have to fit perfectly just then or maybe ever.

She pondered if she had only tried to change to please Lawrence? She thought of how she treated Holland and knew she hadn't changed too much. She wondered if it was possible to erase parts of who she was, even to please someone she loved.

Melody knew she would always love Lawrence, but it would be foolish to continue to hope that her changes would make him love her back like she loved him.

She remembered how Lawrence and Holland lit up around each other, and wondered once again what he saw in her. She would love to take care of things with that girl. She would love to make Lawrence know what an idiot he was. How completely stupid he seemed when he was around Holland.

It felt good to tell Lawrence off, even if only in her mind. Melody walked slowly back to Auntie Red's and Uncle Tilden's home.

All the unanswered questions, the unanswered future, all of it felt tolerable, all were protected under a heavy blanket of purity and white.

Chapter Twenty Nine

Christmas Eve felt weird. It felt nice. It seemed a lot of emotions packed into one evening. Holland's mother came out of her room, and that night it seemed like things changed drastically.

She and Luke and their dad stayed busy that afternoon, wrapping presents, preparing the usual Christmas Eve dinner of chimichangas. When their mother emerged from behind the bedroom cell, Holland actually felt a smidge of softheartedness for her.

She walked out dressed, not wearing pajamas, wearing the old Christmas sweatshirt that she had worn for many years on Christmas Eve. She looked very thin and had dark circles under her eyes, but her haired and been washed and curled and the faded sweatshirt was clean. Her jeans hung on her like she needed a belt to hold them up.

Holland's mother stood watching the family, unsure of what to do, of her place in their business. It had to be hard on her, when they noticed her. All their mouths dropped open, even though they all tried to look happy, they only succeeded in looking surprised.

Their mother must have felt like she was a visitor, who walked in without knocking. The visitor understands that they have walked in on something that does not include them.

It was all so obvious it hung in the air, Mother, a visitor in her own home. The Mother, who had been gone so long, that when she stopped in for a visit, well it threw off the usual flow of the home.

"Hi," she said simply to them.

"Hi," they said in unison. Luke was at her side.

Holland could tell her mother sensed the being-a-visitor-in-her-own-home-thing even before Holland did. Holland could see by the look on her face that she sensed it like a two-by-four hitting her hard in the side of her head. Holland felt for sure that she would cry and go back into her room for the rest of the Christmas holidays.

But then an electrifying, unanticipated miracle happened. Her mother, in her completely fragile state, squared
back her shoulders, and smiled at all of them and walked to the
kitchen table and sat down on a chair.

"Um, Mom, do you want to wrap a present or something?" Luke asked, trying not to gawk and act nervous.

"Sure," she said in a little voice, a voice that hadn't
been used much.

Luke and Dad were quickly there with a gift and some
paper and even Holland picked up some tape and put it on the
table in front of her.

What happened next was truly unexpected, and more
abnormal than she, her dad, or Luke trying so hard to act normal. Her mother smiled, giggling at the family. Not the crazy,
out of control laugh, but a natural laugh at their eagerness. Her
laugh was small and quiet at first, but as she sat there watching
their surprised faces, and their intentness to get her wrapping
presents, her laughing intensified.

They all stopped dead in their tracks. They could not
move, could not speak. The three of them only stood numbly

watching her laugh like at them like they were funny, like they had done something truly hilarious, or told the best joke, or, Holland didn't really know what. Her mother seeing the family frozen, laughed even harder. Not the scary, strange laugh from Thanksgiving. She laughed like she knew how, like she was a regular laugher.

Finally, Holland unfroze enough to look over at Luke. He wore a scared expression, like a small child that happened on a big scary dog. Holland knew he worried about a repeat of Thanksgiving. But then she saw once again his goodness come shining through, always there, always just right there.

His face softened and his big heart gushed up into a sweet smile that turned into a sweet laugh. Then he walked over to their mother and put his arms around her and buried his head in her clean, curled hair. She pulled him down and kissed his strawberry head, and continued to laugh.

She looked at Holland, who struggled to know what to feel. Most of all Holland felt blown away with the unexpected-ness of it all, the unpredictability of life.

Most of life feels all so completely predictable on a day to day basis, Holland thought. But just when you get a little comfortable with your routine, whoosh, something happens to change the baseline of how you look at things.

Holland really liked that about life, and she really hated that about life. She stood there not quite able to get a footing on how she felt about it all. Dad put his arm around her. "Don't over-think it Holland. It's Christmas Eve. Enjoy what is."

Holland looked up at him, startled that it came out his mouth, startled that he was so on her wave-length at that moment that her dad knew and understood her. She was startled that anyone could know and understand her, at the wisdom of his advice that she actually did not feel angry, that she wanted to take his advice.

Dad pulled Holland into a hug. She laughed. He laughed. They all laughed like they had been told something funny. They did not seem like the family who moved to Holbrook, Arizona, with a Mother who stayed in her bedroom. They did not seem like the family who had nothing to laugh at, because apparently they did.

Chapter Thirty

Laughter filled the Christmas Eve party and meal. Melody loved the delicious food, and teasing. She didn't love the careful distance kept between Lawrence and her.

The family tradition was that each person could select one gift and at the end of the evening, starting with the youngest, open that gift, saving the rest for Christmas morning.

Melody's turn came right before Lawrence. She looked through the gifts under the tree. A small gift from Lawrence had surprised her. She tried to hide her emotion but her hands shook with excitement as she opened it.

Inside the box lay a beautiful turquoise pendant on a silver chain. Melody sat blinking, not knowing what to say. She finally looked over at Lawrence and smiled. Lawrence breathed a sigh and smiled back.

When it was Lawrence's turn to open a gift he looked through the gifts with his name on them. Melody felt sick she had saved his gift hoping to give it to him alone. She wanted to run to her room and grab the gift so he could open it, but didn't. Lawrence finally settled on a gift from his mom, a pair of sweats.

Later, after everyone left or went to bed, Melody and her mom sat for a long time looking at the Christmas lights. "Are you doing better tonight?" Nascha asked.

"Yeah, I think so," she answered feeling drowsy.

After a while her mom got up, "We better go to bed so Santa can come."

Melody smiled and reluctantly got up and went into the small bedroom she and her mother were using. She crawled into the cold sheets and lay shivering until she warmed things up enough to relax. She thought about her gift for Lawrence and got an idea that made her smile until she fell asleep.

# # #

Christmas morning dawned cold. The storm had blown over and the sun shone brilliantly on the snow.

Lawrence, still half-asleep, heard scratching at his window. He finally worked one eye open to look towards the noise. Melody stood outside the window smiling. She vanished as soon as he saw her.

Lawrence smiled, quickly dressing warmly and tip-toed outside, following Melody's footprints to the wash. She sat on the same log that they had sat on the morning before. He sat next to her, not knowing what to say.

"Lawrence, it's Christmas, how about if we take a holiday from everything?"

"What do you mean?"

"Let's not talk about anything today. Let's just enjoy Christmas."

Melody pulled something out of her jacket, a small box.

Lawrence grinned at her and opened it slowly. It was a black onyx bolo tie. Lawrence started laughing, "It is really nice, Melody." He held it up to a wisp of hair trailing from under her hat. "The stone is the exact color of your hair. But isn't it something for an older man?"

Melody laughed back. "Lawrence, you may only be in the ninth grade but you are the oldest man that I know."

"Just what do you mean by that?" Lawrence asked, thinking about the gift that Holland had given him before Christmas break, and the news he hoped his mother would talk to him about.

"You are not like a normal guy your age and you know it!" Melody replied. "You are already acting like president of the Navajo Nation!"

"Yeah, and as president, I declare you number one squaw," he said, feeling happiness overtake his thoughts.

"Okay, and as first squaw of the Navajo, you better follow my every command."

"What is your every command?" he asked.

"First is that you come down and just be Ninth-Grade-Lawrence, not President of the Navajo-Nation-Lawrence. Just for today?"

"Okay," he laughed, "just what would Ninth-Grade-Lawrence do differently?"

"Well, he would know a nice, ninth-grade Navajo girl when he was around her and not try to figure out what she would be like at thirty!"

Lawrence admired Melody's spunk and pretty face; he

grabbed her around the waist, smiled at her shocked face and kissed her, softly and fiercely at the same time. He stayed close and leaned his forehead against hers, distinctly aware of his heart in his chest.

"Is that what a ninth-grade boy would do?" she asked shyly.

"Yes, a ninth-grade boy would want to do just that."

"I can feel my heart beat between my ears," she said in wonder.

"I'm pretty sure that my heart is aware of this," he smiled.

Melody laughed and turned and started running. He picked up a big snow ball and plowed her in the back. She ran up out of the wash to Lawrence's home where Christmas breakfast was being prepared.

A few moments later Lawrence walked in trying to act casual, but all could tell he did not pull it off in the least. Holding up his bolo tie, he announced overly loud, "Hey look what I got for Christmas!"

Lawrence's mom, Antonia, looked surprised. His animated voice brought a smile to her worried face and those were hard to come by some days. Lawrence, seeing his mom

smile, walked over and planted a big kiss on her cheek. The

unusual display of affection made even grandma smile.

Lawrence seeing her reaction planted another big kiss on

grandma's cheek.

Henry, watching the whole scene, said, "Looks like

Santa did come after all." Everyone erupted into laughter.

Chapter Thirty One

"Holland, Holland wake up! It's Christmas morning!" Luke sat on the edge of her bed, shaking her gently.

Holland didn't open her eyes. "What time is it?" she moaned, feeling worry of what her mother could be up to.

"It's dawn, hurry, Mom and Dad are waiting for us," he said with more urgency.

"Mother?" Holland said working one eye open. It still looked dark outside. "Our mother is going to make a show two days in a row? Wow, it must be Christmas or something."

Luke giggled nervously. "Shh, she'll hear you. Get up!"

She stumbled out of bed, grabbing a sweatshirt and pulling it over her pajamas she followed Luke into the living room.

They were all grumbling inside, but none of them would have thought about grumbling aloud to Luke, whose eyes were shining as bright as the Christmas tree lights. None of them could help but smile and play along.

Each took turns opening gifts. Luke dug under the tree, seeming to come up with an endless supply of them. He handed Holland a small box. Her heart pounded, it was from Lawrence. She honestly did not know that Lawrence had given her a gift.

"How?" Holland mouthed to Luke. Luke smiled gleefully. She cringed inside, because she spent about two weeks debating whether or not to give Lawrence a gift. She had finally decided. On a piece of card stock she had written in her best writing, her favorite quote, the one from Agatha Christie.

Holland framed and wrapped it and found a moment with Lawrence alone after school, a few days before Christmas break. As he unwrapped it, she had died a thousand deaths questioning the gift. She worried the quote that inspired her so much, would sound old, and pessimistic, and weird.

Lawrence had opened the gift and smiled. Softly, he read and reread the quote. He started nodding in the affirmative. He gave Holland a look of kindness and told her he loved the quote. He said it was a good thing for him to remember, especially at this time.

His look of tenderness touched Holland right down to the core. But his statement let her know that he had a whole, big, full-blown life that she knew nothing about. His statement let her know that he was dealing with something right then and there, something she knew nothing about.

Holland cringed again sitting there on Christmas morning, sitting in her strange world that he knew nothing about, wondering about his world.

"Are you going to open it, or just sit there and think?" Luke said impatiently. She slowly opened the small box. Inside lay a beautiful turquoise and silver ring. It looked like an old ring. Like it had been worn and taken care of for years. A ring. Her mind was ringing. And then a stern warning from herself. Don't read into a ring.

Holland put it on her ring finger. It was too large. She put it on her middle finger and it fit perfectly. Holland had never been one to wear any jewelry so the ring looked different.

Her mother interrupted her thoughts, "It looks beautiful

with your red hair."

She looked up to see her mother studying her. Her mother wore a surprised look, like she had not seen Holland in months. Her mother's eyes were big and soft, and Holland could see she had taken in her every expression for the past few moments. It seemed as if she realized Holland had a whole life going on in Holbrook that she knew nothing about and felt suddenly curious.

She looked at her mother and smiled. She placed her hand with the ring over her heart and patted a few times. Her mother who had been gone for so long, and would soon be gone again, seemed totally with her at that moment. Her moth er took her own hand and placed it over her heart and patted a few times.

Later on Christmas morning, Holland climbed back in her bed thinking about the day so far. It actually felt okay. In some ways it even felt huge. Huge because she had actually been around her family enough to start catching on to some stuff, that until then, she had somehow missed.

Holland felt sure she missed it because of her deliber-ate-head-first-dive into school. That could be the only reason, her being so perceptive and all.

Holland thought that the family could go on in dysfunc-tion for an infinite amount of time. At least it felt like they had done so, and they could continue to do so.

But the Christmas Eve laughing party, and being to-gether Christmas morning, acting normal, proved that all wrong. The normal routine of her mother in her bedroom was upturned and Holland felt begrudging respect for her mother's ability to fight through whatever it was she needed to fight through to be a part of the holidays.

The biggest thing Holland had caught on to over the break was that things were brewing between her mother and dad. It still seemed all quite subtle. She even wondered if her parents were catching on to it themselves. But maybe she was being condescending.

But what Holland really saw brewing was her mother stirring enough to make some kind of move. She had graduat-ed from no function, to poor function. Enough function that her brain kicked into gear and her brain told her to do something, anything, just move. Maybe it was condescending to think that she caught on to it before her parents, but Holland could see it clear as day.

Her dad's attitude towards her mother seemed to be pushing her silently. He seemed to yell silently, "Yes do something, do something even if it tears up the family. Nothing could be more destructive than living like we have been." Her dad seemed to be saying that with every gesture, every look. He spoke it all without speaking one word. And Holland truly wondered if her dad even knew he said it.

Holland wondered long and hard if Luke could hear it all. She hoped he could, and hoped he couldn't. She wanted to give him a heads up, but she, just like her parents, did not say a word, just continued to wait and see.

Holland knew Luke was smart, maybe way smarter than she was. He just had the handicap of smarts combined with niceness. She wondered what in the world does someone do with smarts and niceness together. What can that combination ever amount to?

After a while her intense analyzing made her sleepy and she fell asleep. But during the break, her mother continued coming out of her room every day. Coming out for a while and interacting with the family. Holland felt she could only sit back and watch where it led.

Chapter Thirty Two

In the middle of January, Lawrence sat in English feeling sleepy and bored. He hardly took his eyes off the back of Melody's head, a few rows forward. He berated himself for sitting behind her. Watching Melody, and thinking about Christmas vacation, Lawrence could hardly concentrate on anything else. It made him uneasy to keep reliving his time in the wash with her.

Lawrence felt completely at a loss as to know how to sort things out. He knew things were not going well with his mother. On the last day of the break, his mom had finally told him.

She'd found him in his room and sat on his bed, "Lawrence, do you have a minute?" She was nervous.

Lawrence felt a shake within him. He knew what was coming.

"I have something I need to tell you." Tears clouded her beautiful black eyes. She hastily wiped them away, "Lawrence I have some news to tell you that is not good."

Lawrence sat and put his arm around her, not knowing whether to tell her he already knew, or let her say it. As he fumbled through his mind for the answer, she said quietly, "I have cancer."

Lawrence gulped and looked at her. Coming from her it seemed more real than it ever had. "But I feel quite sure it will all be okay and that everything will get taken care of. I don't want you to worry." His mother fought to hold her tears in.

"Mom," Lawrence could not think of a single word to add to it.

His mother buried her face in his shoulder. Neither could speak. After a few minutes she squeezed his arm and left the room, leaving him sitting on the bed feeling numb.

They did not speak of it again. It felt great to be home, around family, around Melody. But his parent's worry seemed to fill every corner of the house.

Then the whole thing with Melody happened. He won-

dered about an interaction with Melody on a level that serious.

Lawrence felt more and more entangled with her, with less of

an ability to free himself. It felt like those dreams when he tried

to run and couldn't. And, he thought ruefully, his attempts at

running were pathetic.

The family had been snowed in the entire week after

Christmas. He'd played with Melody and his cousins in the

snow for hours. Laughing, talking, it was probably the best time

Lawrence ever had, and the hardest. Fearful for his mother,

fearful of the fear he saw his parents experiencing, having fun

with Melody, but worrying about it. None of it made sense.

Back in school, staring at Melody's back seemed to

cap off Lawrence's frustration. He pulled his eyes away and

looked at the desk next to him. There sat Holland watching

him. Lawrence smiled, happy for the distraction. Holland smiled

back and ducked her beautiful red head, blushing.

Lawrence sat staring openly at her, which for a Navajo

was considered rude, but at the moment Lawrence could care

less. He looked at the turquoise ring on her middle finger. He

looked at her captivating face and beautiful hair. He never felt fearful with Holland.

"Why do you watch Melody like that? Holland whispered, surprising him with her perceptiveness and boldness.

Lawrence fumbled for an answer, wondering about that himself. Before he could answer, she continued, "What is it about her?"

He looked at Holland, and saw that she did not ask it maliciously, she only asked it out of curiosity. She could see.

"I'm not watching her," Lawrence's attempts at lying were poor, and he could see Holland's reaction of hurt as she looked down and bit on her lower lip.

"I mean, I don't want to watch her. I'm just thinking I guess."

Holland looked at him, her eyes held the question. "Thinking about what?" But she did not say it aloud. Finally, she said, "I don't really have a right to know. I mean to ask you about it, I can just see it and I wonder about it. I mean, what you say about her, and how you look at her are two different things, that's all, that's all I'm trying to say."

Lawrence say frustration swell up in her, reminding him uncannily of the times he saw it swell up in Melody, "It's not really my business to ask anyway." She looked away, chewing heavily on her lips.

Lawrence reached under the table and took her hand, he squeezed it tightly. Holland looked over at him, quit chewing on her lip, and smiled.

# # #

Melody sat in English, wondering about Lawrence, wondering if he watched her, wondering if he thought about Christmas break as much as she did.

From the moment that Melody had been back to school, Troy had been pressuring her—for what she could not quite figure out. That morning, as she crossed the street to the high school, he had magically appeared at her side.

"Hey, beautiful!" Troy, as always, seemed clueless and his voice became pouty. "How come we are not hanging out more?"

Melody stopped walking and stared at him. She usually tried to laugh and joke her way out of it, but Troy was so dumb it felt pointless sometimes. She had learned that getting angry and telling him off only seemed to strengthen his resolve.

Melody thought about Toshee, who had backed off during the entire fall semester and now seemed to have a re-newed energy of hate, harassing her in veiled comments.

"Troy, whatever you did before to have Toshee back off, well, I'd appreciate it if you could get her to leave me alone again."

Troy smirked, "I can do it again, I will be happy to do it again, but only for a price."

Melody rolled her eyes in disbelief, turned and marched away, not waiting to hear what the price would be.

The New Year felt like a disaster so far. Melody tried to talk to Lawrence a few times since they started back to school. He was overly nice, but a closed book.

"What is it with guys?" she muttered quietly to herself, and tried to concentrate on English.

Chapter Thirty Three

After school, Holland closed her locker after last peri-
od. She turned, and right next to her stood Melody. Holland felt
the color drain from her already pale cheeks.

Melody looked at her with an intensity of hate that she
recognized well. Holland understood that depth of emotion.
Something deep inside of Holland welled up with that same
intensity of hate and anger. Rage filled right up to the top of
her. Holland did not care if she got the smack beat out of her.
She would go down with a fight.

"What do you want?" Holland asked in her snarliest
voice. Hoping like heck it sounded as mean as she felt, as she
knew she was.

Holland saw Melody's eyes flicker for the smallest second in surprise, which filled Holland with even more drive. At that moment she wanted to intimidate Melody like she had been intimidated, eye for an eye.

Melody brought her surprise under control and replied coldly, "Nothing, I want nothing from you."

"Why are you standing so close to me looking that way?" Holland hoped her voice sounded menacing.

"How long are you going to be here?" Melody asked coldly.

"Why does it matter?"

"I want you gone," Melody answered, her face close.

Holland purposely took her hand with the turquoise ring and combed her fingers through her hair. Melody saw it and pulled a chain with a turquoise pennant out from under her shirt.

Holland looked at the pennant and understood where it came from. The pennant and the memory of Lawrence watching Melody so intently during first hour threw her off her sureness. She wavered in her anger.

Melody took a step closer to Holland, so near a book would not have fit between them. Lawrence rounded the corner and saw. He walked up to Holland, ignoring Melody, and took her by the arm, pulling her away. As he pulled he spoke loud enough for everyone to hear.

"Holland, I was just looking for you, wondering if you would come to a ceremony with me this weekend, a ceremony of healing for my mother."

Holland blinked. She looked at Melody. Melody looked like she had been hit in the stomach. She turned and ran down the hall.

Somehow Holland understood Melody knew that the invitation to the ceremony was coming and felt betrayed, so the reason for the confrontation.

Holland's head was spinning from the cascade of emotions, the anger, the fear, the surprise, the knowledge that Lawrence believed Melody was the only aggressor in that scene. It took Holland a moment to clear her brain. Lawrence sat watching. Holland could tell he assumed she felt completely afraid.

Lawrence put his arm around her, which caused further unclear thinking, but felt really, really good. Finally, Holland's honesty got the better of her.

"What you just saw Lawrence. That was me too."

Lawrence looked above her, at some far off thing he could not see. "I figured that, but I know her, know how she works."

"I would love to go with you, but I don't want you asking me because you feel sorry for me," she said, struck with a sudden thought, wondering if he asked her to make Melody jealous. "But I would still love to go. Just don't feel like you have to be my one-man social committee or something."

Lawrence smiled at her. A stunning smile, Holland thought. "No, I won't make you my charity case. I don't think you need my charity. Melody probably heard that I was going to do this because I had to get permission before I asked you. But you need to understand that this is not a social event. It is a ceremony for healing, for my mom. I don't know if you know, but my mom has cancer and started chemotherapy." he said the word 'chemotherapy' like it was a big, painful word.

Holland blanched. It sent a shockwave down through her.

"I'm so sorry," The words sounded light, but Holland couldn't find more.

"Thanks," Lawrence too was at a loss for words.

They stood for a few moments, neither speaking.

"Well I better go. Luke will be waiting," Holland said quietly. She felt awkward, but reached up and hugged Lawrence.

"Thanks," he said again.

Holland turned to leave.

"Wait. Can I come over to your house for a little while?" Lawrence asked almost apologetically.

Holland felt a sinking feeling, "Um, yeah, sure."

Lawrence picked up on her hesitation, "If it's not a good time it's okay."

Holland breathed deeply. She would just have to make it work, "No, it would be great. Um, my mother, well my mother is probably in her room. She's been sick.

"Sick? Maybe it's not a good time."

"No, come, please. She's been sick a lot, well sometimes lately."

They walked out to the street to find Luke, standing on the corner waiting.

"Hey Luke, Lawrence is coming over for a while. I told

him our mother might be in her room, because she's been a little sick," Holland said trying to give Luke the eye and explain it all with a look.

As they walked home, she wondered about Lawrence's mom. What was she like? What kind of Mom was she? Holland wondered if her mother got cancer, what it would be like. Would she come out of her room?

"Yeah, Lawrence, this is basically what she's like. She gets lost in her thoughts," Luke said matter of fact.

"I can see that," Lawrence said smiling.

Holland felt embarrassed, "I'm sorry, Lawrence. I can't quit thinking about what you told me about your mother."

Lawrence looked at Luke and said quietly, "I just told her my mother has cancer."

"Oh, wow," Luke answered softly.

"It's hard, it's hard when your mother isn't doing so well," Holland said, taking Lawrence's hand.

Lawrence smiled. "Well she just started the treatments, so it's like she is still herself. Well, she hasn't really been herself. She's been kind of distant . . ."

Holland wondered what her mother's being herself

would seem like. She couldn't remember for sure.

Inside the house Holland breathed a sigh of relief. Things didn't look too bad and her mother was nowhere in sight.

"Do you want a Coke or something?" Luke asked Lawrence.

"Yeah, sounds great."

As Luke handed Lawrence a Coke, he said, "Hey, I have this cool book about Navajos. Come to my room; I'll show you."

Lawrence laughed, "You want to show a Navajo a book about Navajos?"

"Yeah, you can fact check it for me," Luke was smiling broadly.

Holland stood and watched the two quickly becoming friends. "Well I'll just go clean the bathroom," she joked.

Neither laughed, they were already headed down the hall to Luke's bedroom. She followed them and sat on Luke's bed. Listening to them go through the book, talking and laughing.

"What's a ceremony?" Luke asked, turning a page.

Lawrence looked at Holland, "Well it's something a medicine man performs for many different occasions. Actually, I've asked Holland to come to one, a healing ceremony for my mother."

"Lawrence, a kid at school was telling me there are bad medicine men too," Luke said.

Holland saw the man at the train wreck smiling at her and shivered.

"Well, yes, that is true," Lawrence said in a way that made her shiver again. "But most of them are good men that want to help people. But definitely, definitely there are evil ones out there. You have to be careful."

"Well how would you know?" Luke asked, in awe.

"Aw come on guys, let's go listen to some music," Holland broke in.

Lawrence and Luke stopped talking and looked at her. "Let's not talk about stuff we don't even know is real or not," she continued.

Lawrence looked at her in surprise. "It's not a matter of if it's real or not," he said quietly, looking at her intently.

Holland got up and walked down the hall into her room

and put some music on. Lawrence and Luke followed her. Holland knew it felt a little uncomfortable, but not as uncomfortable as talking about superstitious maybes. She pushed the man at the train wreck out of her mind.

That night, after Lawrence went back to the dorm, Holland crawled into bed thinking. She realized it is a curse to think at night, to live and relive, then relive once more the conversations of the day. A curse to think them through, wonder about things you didn't hear said. Wonder about motives, feelings. Things you mostly don't get answers to. Welcome to Holland's world, she thought ruefully.

Chapter Thirty Four

The weekend could not come soon enough, yet Holland felt nervous about it coming. She worried about Lawrence's mom, what she would be like, how sick was she. She wondered a lot about the ceremony.

Her dad at first shook his head no when she asked if she could go to Lawrence's home for the weekend. But after she explained about the ceremony, the situation, how completely sure she felt of Lawrence, after telling him about five times, he relented. She asked her dad to be home when Luke got home from school, he nodded.

Friday, after school, Holland grabbed her backpack that held a change of clothes and few necessities. Her heart pounded as she walked as quickly as she could across the street to the dorm. Lawrence stood outside, waiting for her. Lawrence the Beautiful, Holland thought. She felt her face grow red as she approached him and hated it.

"Hi," she said feeling apprehensive.

"Hi, I just have to grab my bag." He took her by the hand and led her inside the dorm.

Inside, she felt transported much farther than across the street of the high school. Navajo kids milled around, filling the halls, getting ready to leave to go home to the reservation for the weekend.

Inside his room, a cowboy looking guy sat on one of the chairs.

"Well, well, well, just who do we have here?" the cowboy asked Holland, smiling.

His friendly manner immediately put Holland at ease, "Hi, I'm Holland."

"I'm Cody," The cowboy shook her hand. His hands felt rough and calloused. Talking to her, but smiling at Lawrence, he said, "I would be a little more careful of the company you keep."

"Yeah, probably right," Holland replied, causing Cody

to laugh.

"Yeah, that is right. Do you even know this guy? I'd be a little worried if I were you, going to his home for the weekend," Cody continued his tease.

"Oh I think she'll be safer with me than she would be with you," Lawrence interjected. "Cody imagines himself quite the ladies' man," Lawrence added.

Cody put a shoe in his bag. "No, I'm not a ladies' man. I'm only interested in one lady." With that he looked at Lawrence and shrugged.

Lawrence looked hard at Cody. Holland wondered what she was missing. Lawrence and Holland left the room and walked out to the bus. Climbing aboard, Holland's heart pounded as she looked down the aisle. She was the only non-Navajo on the bus. As she scanned the bus, she spotted Melody, who sat staring. Eyes full of hate. Holland quickly looked away.

Sitting next to Lawrence on a bus, going home with him for the weekend for a Navajo ceremony for his mom, who had cancer, with a girl a few seats back who despised her, was almost more than Holland could take.

Holland looked at Lawrence after the bus got going. She smiled and hoped her face did not get too red. She had to ask, "Will Melody be at the ceremony?" Trying to sound casual.

"Yes," Lawrence sounded a little uncomfortable. Then turned his head to look out the window.

Holland swallowed a lump that felt much bigger than her throat. Lawrence turned back and took her hand. "I am glad you will be there," he said quietly.

"I'm really glad to get to be there," she said, trying not to sound as eager as she felt. She truly felt in heaven sitting on the bus holding his hand. Holland hoped Melody couldn't see their hands, but hoped she could too.

During the couple of hours, as they sat holding hands, saying little, Holland looked out the window. The landscape of juniper trees, and painted sand, suddenly looked like the most beautiful scenery Holland had ever seen. There were a few patches of snow still clinging to the ground in the shady spots, but Holland had learned that in this part of Arizona, snow came, but didn't always stick around long.

At Lawrence's stop, Melody, Holland, and Lawrence got off the bus. It was chilly, the sun just setting on the horizon.

The half-mile walk down the dirt road was filled with awkward silence. Lawrence no longer held her hand. Holland didn't have anything to say. No one said a word.

Lawrence's house was first in a little group of two homes and a hogan. Lawrence's home was small, but had a front porch that ran the length of it. Lawrence took Holland by the arm as if to say, it was their stop. But he was looking at Melody. "Good night, Melody."

Melody walked on, not answering.

Inside, Holland noticed two things. The home looked immaculate, so clean. But she noticed more how homey it felt. Lawrence's parents were standing at the kitchen table.

Holland thought Lawrence's mother was beautiful, that from her Lawrence got his good looks. As she studied Lawrence's mom she didn't even try not to stare. She wore her black hair pulled back into a thick pony tail, beautiful shiny hair with no grey, with lovely black shiny eyes. She wore dangly turquoise earrings.

Lawrence's dad wore his hair cut short like Lawrence and Holland thought his face held the look of a reserved man.

"Mom, Dad, this is Holland."

"So happy to meet you," Antonia came forward and gave Holland a small hug.

"Hello, Holland," Henry said extending his hand.

"Hi. Thanks so much for having me," Holland said shaking Lawrence's father's hand.

"Hope you two are hungry, supper's ready," Antonia said.

The table was set, and the house smelled wonderful. After washing up, they sat down to a meal of Navajo tacos.

Until that night Holland had never eaten one, never heard of one. They consisted of scone-like bread called fry bread. The bread, first covered with pinto bean chili, then layered with tomatoes, lettuce, and shredded cheese, and topped with salsa. They tasted delicious.

During dinner, no one spoke much, but it felt obvious to Holland the love in the family.

For dessert they had another piece of fry bread covered with cinnamon and honey, which was even more delicious.

Finally, after dinner, Antonia spoke, "Holland, tell us about your family."

Holland gulped and wondered what to tell, "Well my Dad works at the mine, and I have a little brother in the fifth grade; his name is Luke."

"How long have you been in Holbrook?" Henry asked.

"Not long. We moved a few weeks before school started."

"Were you here before the train wreck?" Lawrence suddenly wondered.

"Yes," she said hesitantly. "Actually, my brother Luke, he, he saw it. We were right next to it when it happened."

"Really?" asked Lawrence, looking at his Dad.

"Really," She needed to change the subject and turned to Antonia. "I was so sorry to hear about your . . . your sickness."

Antonia smiled. "That is kind of you to say, Holland. I am very hopeful," she said without looking hopeful.

Everyone went to bed early because the ceremony started at dawn. Antonia told Holland to sleep in Lawrence's bed. He would sleep on a cot in a small room that looked like an enclosed back porch. Holland felt embarrassed to take his bed, but Lawrence insisted also. Holland hurried and got ready for sleep.

As she left the bathroom, Lawrence stood in the hall-way waiting. He looked at Holland in her pajamas but did not say anything, just smiled. Her heart pounded. As much as her heart had pounded that day, she would probably have a heart attack.

Holland smiled back and went into his room and closed the door. She crawled into Lawrence Yellowhair's bed. It smelled clean and felt comfortable.

Even though she felt exhausted her mind raced for a while, reliving everything about the day. She decided to go qui-etly into the kitchen and get a drink of water. As she walked into the kitchen, she stood deciding if she could see well enough to get the drink without turning on the light.

"Holland," Lawrence said quietly. "What do you need?"

She could see him sitting at the kitchen table.

"A drink of water."

"Come here."

Holland walked slowly to where he sat. He pulled her down on his lap and wrapped his arms around her. "Thanks for coming," he said gently.

Holland didn't want to say anything, she felt afraid she would bumble it and ruin the moment.

After a few moments he stood up with her and walked to a cabinet and got a glass and to the sink and filled it with water and handed it to her.

"Thanks for everything," she whispered.

"Good night," he said, and led her down the hall to his room. She was glad he couldn't see the warmth she could feel on her face. He walked away to his cot on the porch.

Chapter Thirty Five

Do dreams mean anything? Holland wondered. The word dream itself kind of doesn't take itself seriously. A dream, a dream-like state. The dream Holland had been dreaming, when Lawrence knocked on the bedroom door the next morning to wake her up, felt unexplainable.

She was full-blown in the dream when he knocked. She dreamed she was walking along a really sandy path with Melody, Melody of all people. They were walking and talking. Holland remembered looking over at her and smiling and Melody was smiling back and it seemed they were that close, with some kind of understanding of each other.

In the dream they were talking about their mothers of all things. It seemed like they were comparing notes, mom notes. Holland couldn't remember a thing Melody told her. But Holland did remember telling Melody about the history with her mother, or without her mother, depending on how one decided to look at it.

Then somewhere in the back of Holland's mind she heard knocking. She left the sandy path and her new friend, and stirred. She opened her eyes. The day dawned brand new, but it felt already as different as any day Holland had ever ex-perienced.

Lawrence opened the door and smiled and her. "Hurry," was all he said and shut the door.

Holland hurried and dressed and pulled her hair into a ponytail. Lawrence was waiting for her. They smiled nervously. He told her to put on a jacket because it was chilly, that they needed to hurry.

He grabbed her hand and they ran down the dirt road towards the hogan. The air was cold and fresh. The smell of the cedar trees and sagebrush made Holland's mouth water a bit.

A small group of people gathered near the front door of the hogan. The only ones that Holland recognized were

Melody, and Lawrence's parents. A man dressed in beige, loose fitting pants, with a burgundy colored velvet tunic, belted at the waist by a beautiful silver and turquoise belt, stood in the doorway holding a basket containing several bundles.

The man started singing. Holland recognized the Navajo language, but could pick out only a few words. As the singing continued, Holland glanced around the group. She decided who must be Auntie Red, Uncle Tilden, Sage, and Tilden Jr. They glanced curiously at her.

Melody and a woman, who must have been her mom, stood close by. Melody looked uptight and hurt.

Just having the dream about her a few minutes before, Holland felt a strange kinship to her, knowing full well it made absolutely no sense.

Lawrence leaned in and whispered in her ear, which was all perfectly wonderful. "The man singing is the medicine man. He is doing a ceremony called the 'Blessing Way.'"

The medicine man placed twigs of oak at the door. Lawrence whispered again. "He is praying through the song, letting the Holy People realize that the hogan will be used for a chant."

Holland wondered who the Holy People were.

Antonia came forward. The medicine man opened a few bundles from his basket.

"That's a buckskin thong. It whirls to sound like thunder, to intimidate evil. Those small-feathered wands are used to protect."

In a few moments Lawrence whispered, "The medicine man is doing an unraveling; it symbolizes releasing my mother from danger".

When the sun started to peak over the horizon, Lawrence told her some offerings were left for the Holy People.

"Who are the Holy People?" Melody asked.

"The Navajo believe there are two classes of people, the Holy People, who are the First Man and First Woman, and others. They created the sun, moon, stars and seasons, and the Earth People, who are us."

When the group started to disperse, Lawrence pulled on Holland's arm and introduced her to his grandmother and grandfather, and aunt and uncle. They smiled at Holland curiously, but little speaking took place. Holland noticed that Lawrence and Melody were careful to stay away from each other.

Lawrence explained that the first part of the ceremony was over, but that it would go on for the rest of the day. As Lawrence and Holland stood talking, Holland noticed a large deep wash running parallel to the three homes. She left Lawrence's side and walked to the edge of it to get a better look.

Lawrence nervously intercepted her, "Let's go get some breakfast. My Auntie Red is having everyone over."

"Okay, I'm just going to look. This wash looks so cool."

Lawrence took Holland's arm, pulling her away. She looked at him, surprised at the look on his face, like a cat on a hot tin roof.

"Is there some reason we are not supposed to go down there?"

"No, no reason. I actually grew up playing in that wash," he said, still acting nervous.

"Wow, I bet it was fun. Let's go explore it."

Lawrence looked over towards his Auntie Red's house. Holland looked over too. She could see Melody standing on the porch watching them. Suddenly, Holland understood something that made her heart ache. She understood that the wash was his and Melody's territory as children. It was their wash. She understood that Lawrence was protecting that.

Holland had never been much for jealousy, well, until the past year. She really hadn't ever been in a situation that warranted jealousy. But being with Lawrence, understanding about the wash, the story of Lawrence and Melody unfolding more and more, Holland felt jealousy creeping in, into every cell, every pore.

Lawrence invited her to come for the weekend, but she was filled with envy of the childhood he spent with Melody. The childhood that did not, could not include her. Whatever happened, Lawrence intended to protect it.

Holland looked at Lawrence. He studied her face. Strangely enough, Holland knew that Lawrence read her just then, read her like a book. He understood her thought process and the emotions it produced. He understood it all.

But Lawrence did not look at her with anger or frustration. He looked at her with tenderness, the tenderness of knowing her thoughts, understanding them and feeling them.

For Holland, this was getting sweeter and more bitter,

lovelier and worse. She glanced over at the wash again. Then it hit her. Down in the wash was the path. The path she saw in her dream. The path she and Melody had walked on. Holland looked over at the house where Melody stood on the porch. Holland could feel her hate from there.

Lawrence interrupted her thoughts, "Wow, you are doing some heavy thinking there."

She didn't want to tell him, but couldn't stop herself.

"Lawrence, I was having this really weird dream when you woke me up this morning. In my dream I was walking down a path with Melody. We were like friends, really good friends. I'm pretty sure the path was in that wash," she said.

Lawrence showed a mixture of emotions on his face. He smiled and shook his head. Holland felt sure it sounded as ludicrous, to him as it did to her. But his eyes were serious.

"Dreams that are had on important occasions usually mean something," he said it in his old person voice.

Holland grimaced. "Yeah, right! Like she will ever be my friend, especially after this weekend. And Lawrence, I know this sounds really hokey, but sometimes I have dreams."

Lawrence smiled and glanced over at the porch, where

Melody still watched. "Holland Adams," was all he said. She looked at him waiting for the rest, but there was no more.

They walked towards his auntie's house. Melody went into the house and Holland did not see her during the break-fast. Holland didn't think the breakfast would be considered Navajo, but it was divine, scrambled eggs, fried potatoes, pan-cakes, sausage and bacon.

Lawrence acted uneasy, like he felt nervous to have her there with his family. But because of how kind everyone treated her, Holland's only nervousness was that Melody sat in a bedroom somewhere hating her guts. Holland felt elated to be with Lawrence, experiencing his life a little, despite the jeal-ously she felt for Melody, and Melody must feel for her.

After the breakfast, they went back to the front door of the hogan. The medicine man was doing a sand painting on the ground. Antonia sat in the painting, leaning against the hogan. Lawrence whispered that the women would leave for a while. That wet sand would be placed on Antonia, changing her from an Earth Person to a Holy Person for a time, so that heal-ing could begin.

Holland walked back into Lawrence's empty house.

She decided to take a bath. She ran the steaming water then sat in the tub and allowed herself to ponder the day.

The ceremony was different than anything she had ever experienced it, yet in a strange way it made sense to her. Her dream felt crazy, but she had dreamt a few dreams before that seemed just as impossible and then things played out just like the dream.

The times before, when her dreams happened, had felt so weird that Holland didn't tell anyone, and honestly tried not to think about them. But today, it didn't seem as crazy that she had dreams. It somehow seemed okay.

Holland thought that through, wondering what she could do, if Melody would even talk to her if she tried. It was obvious Melody had felt for much longer, and probably much stronger, the emotions Holland was beginning to feel for Lawrence. Holland did not blame Melody for hating her.

Why did life have to be so convoluted? She thought as she ducked her head under the water, her hair flaring into a halo of red around her.

Holland dressed and sat on the top step of the porch, letting the sun dry her hair. The small group of men and Antonia were still in front of the hogan. Every once in a while Holland could hear the medicine man sing or chant. She thought of Melody more. She remembered the jealously she felt about the wash. She thought of the dream.

It was all too much to sort through. Her thoughts became hazy and disjointed. Sitting in the warm sun her hair dried and she became relaxed and sleepy. Holland got up, longing for a nap. She walked into Lawrence's room and lay on his bed and fell asleep.

Immediately she was dreaming the dream again. She was walking in the wash. Holland saw a baby strapped to a cradle board. The baby was very little, almost new born. Holland knew it was Melody. The baby, left alone, shivered in the cold. Snow was falling.

Holland understood this was the time when Melody had been taken from her mom and given to Auntie Red to raise.

Then Holland saw Melody as a little girl, and felt the conflict of Melody's strong personality with everyone around her, everyone except Lawrence. She saw Lawrence as a little boy playing with Melody. She saw that he loved her. Holland saw them as they grew older, Lawrence trying to help Melody at school. She saw bits and pieces of things that did she did not recognize or understand.

Holland woke up shivering and crying, crying for Melody and wondering why Melody had to go through all those experiences. As Holland lay there, she questioned why, why, why she would be dreaming about Melody.

She thought about her mixed up family and wondered why something like the dream would happen about a girl she barely even knew. It was extraordinary. That it was completely real she did not doubt. She felt curious about what she supposed to do with the information?

She had told Lawrence about the first dream, felt compelled to. But the latest dream felt different. It felt like she had spied on someone's life.

She relived the dream a few times and felt even more confused, wondering again why it happened. Deep in thought, she jumped a mile when Lawrence knocked on the door.

Her hair could have taken flight, from washing it, to drying it in the sun, to sleeping on it. Holland wiped her eyes and opened the door, worried her face was red and that her hair looked like burning bush.

Lawrence took in the sight of her, smiled that beautiful smile. Holland felt a little hole in the pit of her stomach open, letting the air rush through her insides and stir them up, shaking her heart ever so slightly. Lawrence touched her hair. He pulled it up to his nose and smelled it.

Holland's heart shook harder. It was positively, absolutely the most romantic thing any boy had ever done, other than the kiss at Homecoming. It was the only thing any boy had ever done. She felt sure she had a completely silly grin on her face. She closed her eyes to inhale the glorious moment and Lawrence pulled her closer, leaned in and kissed her lightly on the lips.

Holland's eyes shot open in surprise, a blissfully happy smile on her lips. Lawrence gazed at her, like he was taking in every bit of her, her smile, her hair, everything.

"Come back down to the hogan with me," he said. They walked down, just as the sun was ready to set. The medicine man sang some more. Lawrence's mother looked peaceful and content, still sitting in the middle of the sand painting. His father looked tired. Melody gave Holland looks of hate and hurt.

But Holland looked at Melody with different eyes.

She knew that Lawrence's family was wonderful. She wanted so badly for his mom to get well and be okay. Holland could see how much Antonia loved Lawrence. She knew there was something in his home that she had bits and pieces of at times in her own. Holland knew she wanted more of it, but didn't know if that could happen.

Even though Holland felt confused at why the dreams about Melody, the weekend felt like the beginning of her dreams not feeling so unexplainable. She somehow felt more at peace with herself. It was as though a little crack opened up in the universe, a little crack into the place where things happen for a reason, where things make sense.

She had experienced something, an understanding that everything and everyone were connected on levels that most people don't even begin to suspect. Maybe it all had to do with the Holy People.

The rest of the weekend went all too quickly and then it was over and Sunday afternoon came. After hugging Antonia, and shaking Henry's hand, Holland said, "Thank you so much for letting me be here, for including me." Then to Antonia she said, "I really hope that good things happen for you."

"Oh, thank you," Antonia said, seeming touched by Holland's words. "I'm afraid I couldn't be a very hospitable host. But we did enjoy you being here."

"I'm sure none of it was anything you are used to," Henry said tentatively.

"It wasn't," Holland admitted. "But it all felt really nice, really comfortable. I'm so glad I came. I felt like I learned a few things about myself."

"I learned a few things about you too . . . good things," Lawrence said without embarrassment.

His parents looked at each other, his father raising an eyebrow to Antonia's inquisitive face.

When it was time to walk down the dirt road to catch the bus, Holland could see that Melody had already started walking. Holland did not want to leave, didn't want the weekend to end. She feared going back to her everyday life. Despite the hardness of the situation of Lawrence's mother, there was peace there. At home she wouldn't feel that peace.

The bus ride back to Holbrook was quiet. Holland watched Melody, a few seats ahead, thinking about seeing her as a baby, wanting to know the whole story.

Back in Holbrook, Lawrence walked her home. On the front porch he hugged Holland tight. "Thanks for being there," he said quietly.

Holland squeezed him, "It was wonderful."

Later than night, lying in bed, Holland's head was whirling, twirling, sorting and remembering. She felt again she could not possibly have the wherewithal to take it all in.

She felt so absorbed into Lawrence, into his story, she felt almost afraid. Afraid to go further, and more afraid not to.

Chapter Thirty Six

It grew harder for Lawrence to go home every week-end. His mom had started chemo in Flagstaff, where she would stay during the week, getting home Fridays after Lawrence did. Because his dad worked there during the week, he could at least spend the nights with her.

She was as pale as a white man. She cut her hair short and although it went from thick to thin, it did not all fall out. When Lawrence tried to ask how she was doing, it seemed to cause her more pain for her to talk about it with him, for her to know how much he worried.

He went up and sat behind the rock at the football field and shivered in the cold a couple of times. Melody had not been there.

Every day Lawrence felt Melody's coldness and distance. The hurt in her eyes doing the speaking. Lawrence said
hi to her a few times, but she ignored him. He wanted to reach
out to her, and be around her, and at the same time, he didn't
want to. His indecision making him feel crazy.

Sitting next to Holland in Biology a few weeks after the
ceremony, Lawrence asked, "Any more dreams about
Melody?"

Holland looked startled and said, "Well I don't know."

Lawrence wondered at her answer. Holland was always so direct and upfront. "Well yes or no?"

Holland looked away, emotion written in every square
inch of her face.

"Holland, what? Did you have another one?"

Holland sat and seemed to consider speaking, "I had
another one at the ceremony, when I was taking a nap on your
bed. I didn't know if I should tell you or not. I don't know why I
had it or even what it means . . ."

"Will you tell me about it?" Lawrence asked solemnly
as they both tried to look busy doing a lab.

"Well, yes, I guess I could. It just all confuses me. I

mean if I was going to have a dream like that, it seems like should be about my mother, or something big in my life."

"Why about your mother? He asked.

Holland looked even more conflicted. Lawrence could tell the subject made her extremely nervous. "What about your mother?" he asked again, more persistently.

"My mother, my mother, wow Lawrence," she took a deep breath, "I don't know if I can tell you this," Holland said, fear and worry in her voice.

"Why?" he asked. Her confusion was catching.

"It's just . . . it's just that when I saw your family, your mother, that is how I wish mine was, is." The words were quick and quiet.

"But, you and Luke are close. I saw that the first time I saw you."

"We are. He's my best friend. Always has been," Holland nodded.

"Then what about your mother?" Lawrence countered.

"Well, my mother, well I don't feel close, well I used to maybe," she made no sense.

"Just tell me," he said firmly.

Holland closed her eyes and took a deep breath. "I guess . . . I guess, well I don't guess, I know. It's just my mother has depression, really bad, and she stays locked in her bedroom most of the time."

"What?" Lawrence felt confused.

"I never see my mother, well, rarely. She stays in her bedroom. And when she does come out, it is weird and scary. I keep feeling something is going to happen soon to change it all. I think something could be coming, but, right now she's in her bedroom, doing what? I don't know. I don't want to know. It makes me so, so angry sometimes," Holland told him the information, looking down. When she finished, she looked up at him, tears glistening in her lovely eyes.

He tried wrapping his mind around everything Holland had just told him, wanted to understand, but felt at a loss to do so. What he imagined life would be like if his mother stayed in her room, but could not come close.

Lawrence did not know what to do or say. Any words he could think of sounded trite. He really didn't know how it would all turn out so how could he tell her it would all be okay? Holland sat looking at the desk, her hands folded in her lap. He reached over and took her hand and held it.

Chapter Thirty Seven

The next night there was a dance held for dorm stu-

dents in the dormitory's main living area. Melody, for the hun-

dredth time, wishing she had a roommate, walked alone down

the hall into the dance.

She immediately spotted Lawrence talking to Cody.

She felt a slow simmer of anger, but held her head up as she

found a seat against the wall. She hoped to sit and watch,

watch Lawrence without being noticed.

She had no more sat down when Cody spotted her,

and ambled over and asked her to dance. She smiled, glad to

dance with him.

"So, how is the love-sick-over-Lawrence girl?" Cody

asked bluntly, but so pleasantly Melody wasn't mad.

"I think any emotion over Lawrence is a complete waste of time," she said flatly.

"Well, well, well. Just what I was hoping you would figure out," Cody smiled.

Melody smiled back, wanting to believe her own words. Cody was nice looking, and uncomplicated.

"Just what made you see the light?" he persisted.

"I don't know," Melody rolled her eyes and sighed. "It is what it is."

"Is it because he took the white girl to the ceremony for his mom?"

"Yes and no. Could we just talk about something else?" she demanded.

"Sure, anything at all," Cody laughed.

They talked and laughed the entire song. As the song ended, Melody looked at Cody, she really did enjoy him, she felt completely relaxed with him.

After dancing a few songs with Cody, Troy appeared out of thin air asking her to dance. She was in no mood to deal with Troy.

"Just dance one with him, then I will rescue you," Cody

whispered in her ear.

"Come on," Troy grabbed her hand and led her to the dance floor. Melody groaned inwardly when the song was a slow one. Troy was always too close anyways. She tried to avoid eye contact with Troy's over eager stare. The song seemed to go forever.

"So, we never hang out," he said.

"Yeah," she replied looking away.

The next thing she knew, Troy pulled her in, actually grabbed her butt and smashed her body up to his. She could feel his body, what he wanted her to feel. It sickened her. With anger surging through her, she shoved Troy back forcefully.

Troy responded harshly, yanking her arm.

"Just what are you trying to prove? You little slut!" he screamed in her ear.

Before she could even think of what to do next, she almost fell to the floor in shock as Lawrence jumped on Troy's back, wrapping his arms around his neck, choking him. Troy coughed and sputtered but could not yell. Lawrence's grip was locked tight.

Lawrence barked words loudly in Troy's ear as he

choked him tightly, "You creep! You bastard, if you ever touch her again I will kill you!"

Troy's eye's bulged, as he gasped for breath.

Cody appeared, trying to pull Lawrence off Troy, but Lawrence held tight. A few seconds later the dorm aides and Cody were finally able to pull Lawrence off.

Troy immediately turned and shoved Cody, but Cody did not move an inch.

"I wouldn't go there if I were you," Cody said steadily.

Melody felt dazed, they next thing she knew they were all being led down the hall to Mrs. Thomas's office to be questioned. Troy marched in front, acting eager to tell his story. Lawrence and Melody walked side by side, glancing at each other, but not speaking. Cody followed them.

Mrs. Thomas sat and looked at Troy, Cody, Melody, and Lawrence. Finally, she spoke, "So who will tell me what happened?"

Troy quickly answered, "I was just dancing with Melody. We were minding our own business, next thing I know, Lawrence is on my back choking me."

Mrs. Thomas gave Troy a dubious look. Melody shook

her head slightly in disbelief, looking down at her hands. She was still angry over what Troy had done and even more surprised at what Lawrence did.

"Melody, is what Troy is saying true?" Mrs. Thomas turned to her.

Melody scrambled in her mind to decide if she should say anything. What could she tell Mrs. Thomas? She hated Troy, but didn't want to sell out Lawrence.

Mrs. Thomas turned to Lawrence in frustration, "Lawrence, surely this can't be true; I can't believe it of you."

Melody glanced over at Lawrence. Lawrence sat as still as a stone and would not speak.

Troy piped back up, "It's like he just went psycho or something. I have no idea over what!"

Melody shuddered in disgust. Troy had to be the lowest of life forms Melody had ever encountered. Her mind raced as to how to defend Lawrence.

Mrs. Thomas turned to Cody, "So what did you see?"

Cody shrugged his shoulders and looked hard at Melody. "To be honest, I'm regretting that I didn't see it, because I was turned away when it happened. But we both know if Lawrence lost it like that, I mean I've never seen him like that . . . well you can bet Mrs. Thomas that Troy did something."

Troy glared at Cody, but Melody could see that he would not retaliate against Cody; even Troy was smart enough to get that.

Melody breathed deeply, "Mrs. Thomas, Troy was dancing with me, and well, he pushed up against me, and it made me mad. I pushed him away and Lawrence defended me."

"I touched you? In your dreams," Troy yelled.

"Lawrence is this true?" Mrs. Thomas ignored Troy's outburst.

Melody watched Lawrence. His face remained the same, cold as stone.

After several moments Mrs. Thomas shook her head, Lawrence still would not speak, "Lawrence, I am quite sure there is more to this story, but since you do not choose to share your side with me, and fighting is fighting, I have no choice but to suspend you until next Monday.

Lawrence's eyes shot up in surprise at Mrs. Thomas.

Melody knew it was because, until tonight, he had never even come close to being suspended. But still he would not speak.

"And by the way Troy, the same applies for you, suspended until next Monday. You may leave," Mrs. Thomas said, nodding to Troy.

Troy stood up smirking and left. Mrs. Thomas sat looking at Lawrence a few moments more.

Finally, Melody said, "Thanks Lawrence."

Lawrence did not reply or look at her.

"You three are excused," Mrs. Thomas sighed. Lawrence abruptly got up and left. In the hall Cody looked at her with a confused look. She walked back to her room and slammed the door.

Chapter Thirty Eight

A few hours after he was suspended, because his dad was in Flagstaff with his mom, his uncle Tilden came and picked Lawrence up and took him home. Uncle Tilden smiled curiously at Lawrence as they walked with his bag towards the truck.

They got in and Uncle Tilden drove for several miles before speaking. "I know full well that you had a good reason to fight, or you wouldn't have Lawrence," he said, chuckling a little.

Lawrence smiled a grimace and didn't answer. He wanted to say something. He had wanted to say something in Mrs. Thomas's office. He just couldn't sort through his mind enough to decide on what.

Neither said much going home. Lawrence relived what he had watched Troy do to Melody over and over. He became more and more resolute in his anger over it. But the whole incident left him realizing how entangled he was with Melody. It was as if what he had spent his entire life working at not doing did not matter in the least. It had happened anyway. Complete entanglement.

When they finally got to the dirt road, his uncle Tilden asked, "Lawrence do you want to stay with us since your parents are in Flagstaff?"

Lawrence mumbled, "No, I'll be fine. Sorry you had to make the trip, but thanks."

"No problem, didn't think you would want to stay with us. Just offering because of your traumatic night," Uncle Tilden grinned, "Some time you are really going to have to tell me this story."

"There are a few low-life's in this world that just have to be put in their place once in a while," Lawrence smiled back at him. His uncle nodded at him as Lawrence climbed out of the pick-up.

Lawrence entered his dark house, did not turn any

lights on, went in his bedroom and crawled in bed. He felt a strange relief and went straight to sleep. He slept soundly and dreamlessly. He woke late the next morning, feeling lonely.

He got out of bed, still dressed from the night before and walked into the kitchen. It startled him to see his dad sitting at the kitchen table.

They looked at each other, saying nothing. Finally, Lawrence sat at the table next to him. His father nodded slightly, "Lawrence if you fought someone I know you had justification. I just hope you got things done with this one fight."

Lawrence smiled, "I hope I did too Dad, because I don't like fighting much."

His dad grinned, and got up to fix breakfast. Neither spoke until after they ate the full frying pan of fried potatoes and scrambled eggs. Lawrence felt better than he had since the fight.

"Dad, tell me about Mom. It drives me crazy that I don't know."

Henry sat silently thinking and then looked slowly up, "I know it must be hard son, but your mother insists that it be this way."

"Like I am not going to remember that my mother has cancer and worry?" Lawrence snorted.

"I know, I know. It does not make any sense. None of this does," Weariness appeared in his dad's eyes.

Lawrence regretted speaking so sharply, "I don't even know what kind of cancer she has."

"Ovarian."

Lawrence gulped. He knew ovarian was a bad kind of cancer. They were all bad, but Lawrence remembered reading somewhere that ovarian cancer had a low recovery rate. "Do the doctors say they will be able to cure it?"

"They don't know. The chemo is hard, but she is determined."

"I just wish she would let me be part of it."

"She is just doing what she knows how, what she feels is best."

"How are you holding up, Dad?" Lawrence asked, embarrassed to be asking such a personal question of his dad.

"Well, okay, until I hear my son has been fighting at school," Henry said with a small smile.

Lawrence was not surprised that his dad would not

speak of how he was doing. It was the Navajo way. It was also why his dad would not make him explain the fight, or defend it. He would trust Lawrence.

"Take a shower son and let's go to Flagstaff and see your mother. We'll stay with her, and bring her home for the weekend."

Chapter Thirty Nine

Lawrence felt nervous and embarrassed to go back to school the next Monday. There was still a little buzz, and some looks and giggles, but fortunately most of the students had movod on from tho inoidont.

Other than Cody bringing it up every time he saw Lawrence. "Hey when are you going to tell me why you tackled the guy like that? And tell me once again how you don't care about the girl so much?" he said to Lawrence at least five times.

And then, "yeah, you are going to be hurting when she goes for me." But Cody couldn't hide that he loved the fact that Lawrence fought Troy.

Lawrence wondered what would happen when he ran

into Troy, but Troy avoided Lawrence as much as Lawrence avoided Troy.

The weekend with his parents had been comforting. Just knowing what kind of cancer it was, in a strange way, felt consoling. His mother was not doing well and that was obvious. Lawrence comforted himself thinking she was in the middle of chemo, how could she be doing well?

Lawrence did not see Melody until that morning in English. They walked into class at the same time. Melody touched Lawrence's arm, "Are you doing okay?"

Lawrence felt stupid, "Yeah, I think I can handle it."

Melody cringed, "That's not what I meant."

In over his head with embarrassment, Lawrence turned his back to Melody and sat down. Lawrence sat down next to Holland, who looked at him with big questioning eyes. Lawrence wondered if she would still feel the same towards him.

During English Lawrence wondered if Holland would ever get in a fight. He decided that he could see Holland fighting, or trying to fight, for something she really believed in. It made him smile to himself thinking about it. He thought she would fight better verbally than physically. Lawrence glanced over at Holland with a feeling of warmth.

Holland was smart, pretty, and so appealing. He glanced up at Melody's back. The incident with Troy had surprised Lawrence as much as anyone. When he realized what Troy was doing to her, it had stirred up an emotion in him that he still couldn't explain, especially to himself.

Lawrence struggled throughout the day with a blur of emotions about his mother, Melody, and Holland. When the day finally ended, he crossed the street to the dorm. The day felt warm, like winter could be ending. Lawrence decided to go the rock.

As he walked up, he was relieved to see Melody there, "Ya'at'eeh."

"Hello," Melody smiled unsurely, then started talking quickly. "Lawrence, I never thought you couldn't handle it, I hope you don't feel bad about fighting. I mean you probably do, but I, I do appreciate it, I mean . . ."

Lawrence snickered and interrupted her, "I thought that might impress you. I remember all the times you fought in grade school."

Melody looked half amused and half hurt. "Lawrence you know I have given fighting up."

"I know you have, but I still thought it might impress you, did it?" Lawrence answered, wondering why the heck he said it, when he had never thought it.

Melody put her head down, "Is the only reason you did it was to impress me?"

Lawrence, disarmed by her honesty, replied, "No."

Melody looked up and caught his eye, "Well, why then?"

"I saw what happened and I guess it made me a little crazy. Has he bothered you since the dance? If he has you need to tell me."

Melody smiled quietly, "If I told you he was bothering me, what would you do?"

"I don't really know," he admitted, looking Melody straight in the eyes. "But I'd think of something."

"Troy is such a scum bag," she said softly.

"Glad to know you finally see that."

"I guess I kind of knew. I never did like him you know. I really kind of used him too."

"You used him? How?" Lawrence asked, feeling annoyed.

"I liked the attention, especially when I saw you hanging out with Holland."

Lawrence looked at Melody, not sure how to answer, not sure if he even wanted to know how to feel about it all. "Well if you see me talking to Holland again, find a better guy for the attention," Lawrence got up to leave.

Melody felt the same frustration's boiling up in her. She wondered why Lawrence was so stupid to talk to, "Wait Lawrence, I want to know how your mom is doing."

His eyes clouded over, "Not good Melody, not good."

Melody sat in stunned silence, watching Lawrence leave. She put her head on her knees and stabbed heavily at the dirt.

# # #

Late that night there was a soft knock on Melody's dorm door. She stumbled to the door, half-awake. Cody looked at Melody in her pajamas and sighed, and shook his head. "Hey are you awake?"

"Do I look like I'm awake? You woke me up to ask me

that?" she asked half annoyed.

"No, not really," he said rolling his eyes. "Your Mr. Lawrence is in some kind of bad way. I'd rather be coming to your room for any other reason than to tell you to go help him."

Melody swallowed hard and hugged Cody quickly.

"Oh yeah, yeah, almost makes it worth it," he smiled. "He's behind the gym, in a world of hurt, I've been trying to comfort him, but he wants you."

Cody stood at the door, and watched her pull a sweat-shirt over her pajamas, and her running shoes on.

"I'll go find him and thanks Cody." She stopped and put her hand on his shoulder.

Cody looked at her and put his hand on her back. "Now's not the time, but sometime will you come help me when I'm in a bad way?" he said, looking serious.

"Yeah, of course I would, and yeah, now's not the time," she said, liking him even more.

Cody left and she tiptoed down the hall and outside. Lights had gone out long ago and she breathed a sigh of relief when no one saw her leave the dorm.

Lawrence was sitting against the building, curled in a

ball, hugging his knees. Melody hurried to him, sat down beside him, linking her arm through his.

Cody was right; something was wrong, very wrong. Melody could tell that Lawrence was crying.

"Is it your mom? Have you heard something?" Melody asked quietly.

All Lawrence could do was nod. He could not speak. Finally, he composed himself enough to get the words out. "My dad called from Flagstaff. Things are not good. My mother has been in and out of consciousness all day. I can't believe it. I was just with her a few days ago."

Melody's heart sank. She wrapped her arms around him.

"Auntie Red is coming in the morning to take me to Flagstaff," he mumbled miserably.

He sat silently for a few more moments. Then he sniffed and Melody sat back against the wall next to him, again linking her arm through his.

Finally, Lawrence regained his composure. "Melody, will you come to Flagstaff with me? I need you there."

Melody felt surprised, but knew she would go. "I'll have

my mom call Mrs. Thomas. I know it will be okay."

Melody stood and pulled Lawrence up. Melody leaned her head on his shoulder, not wanting to wonder what was ahead. "I'm going to go call my mom and find Mrs. Thomas right now; will you be okay until morning?"

"Yes," was all he said as they walked in and went separate ways back to the dorm.

Chapter Forty

Early the next morning, Lawrence knew he looked as bleary-eyed as Melody did when Auntie Red picked them up. Auntie Red looked worried, and no one talked much. She pulled off the interstate in Winslow and drove through a fast food restaurant. But nobody seemed able to eat.

The sun had not been up very long when they pulled into the hospital parking lot in Flagstaff. Auntie Red explained, "Your mother started a new round of chemo. She had a reaction much more severe and passed out. She comes to, then goes out again, over and over. I'm afraid it's not good," she finished, looking at Lawrence.

Lawrence flinched at the information, but was grateful to be told upfront. He knew it was far more than his dad would share with him.

As they walked out of the elevator and down the hall, Melody took his hand. He squeezed it much harder than he intended. Melody smiled at him, but he felt like running down the hall, out of the hospital.

Quietly, they entered the room. His father stood in the corner. Lawrence could not tell if his mother was unconscious, or sleeping. He felt a dread come over him, none of it seemed real. As they crowded into the tiny room, Antonia opened her eyes and smiled. She motioned for Lawrence and he went and sat on the edge of her bed. Tears rolled down his cheeks and he couldn't think of what to say.

His mother seemed much weaker than just a few days before. But she gazed at him with a look of contentment, and he could feel her love. Lawrence leaned down and rested his head on his mother's shoulder, careful not to put much weight on it.

He felt his mother's devotion roll through the room like a wave. It swirled around her and then into Lawrence. He rec- ognized the experience, but did not know from where. He knew it was sacred.

Lawrence finally looked at his dad, and Melody. Tears streamed down Melody's cheeks. His mother looked at her sister, and at Melody, and then tried to smile bravely.

His dad put his hand on Lawrence's shoulder. "Son, maybe you should give your mother a chance to rest."

Lawrence nodded. He and Melody left, leaving his father and Auntie Red with his mom. They walked silently down the hall and stood waiting for the elevator. The doors opened and they went down and out of the building. A blast of Flagstaff's icy air hit them. The air smelled like pines and their cheeks burned with cold. Lawrence breathed deeply.

They walked down the street. Lawrence turned to Melody, "Do you think my mom will make it?"

Melody looked surprised. "I . . . don't really know. I wish I could tell you she will, but I don't know."

Lawrence nodded. "I know you don't know. I just wish I had someone that could tell me what will happen."

"In Mormon seminary they talk about what happens when you die," Melody hesitated.

"What do Mormons think?" he asked.

"They believe when you die your spirit leaves your

body and goes to heaven. Then someday you get resurrected and your body and spirit go back together and stay together for eternity."

"What do you think?"

"I'm not always sure," Melody answered honestly. "Sometimes when I hear it, it feels right, and sometimes I don't know."

"Do you believe Navajo's beliefs about death?" Lawrence asked.

"I don't completely understand them," she said hesitantly.

"Navajo belief is that the spirit leaves the body at death and begins a journey to the next world, that those left behind showing too much emotion after the death of their loved one might interrupt that spirit's journey to the next world."

"I don't know how you can always control every emotion. I wouldn't want to feel like it was my fault if I interrupted a spirit's journey," she said.

They walked a few more blocks, past neighborhoods of old homes made of lava rock from ancient volcanos. "I really never thought about it, or realized how hard it must have been

for you to be away from your mom all those years," he admitted.

Melody grimaced. "It was hard, but this is kind of different. My mom was gone because she was drinking. Your mom
could be gone because she got sick. But I guess the drinking is
a sickness too . . ."

Lawrence replied honestly, "I guess the only good thing
about your mom being messed up, is that she came back and
now she is sober."

"I try not to, but sometimes I still get scared that she
will go back to drinking."

Lawrence knew the reality of her fear and did not know
what to say.

"She had another relapse when I was in seventh
grade," she revealed quietly. "It was terrible. She left for days
and I was home alone. I didn't tell anyone because I knew they
would take me away from her. But then she did come home
and she felt so terrible." She took a deep breath, closing her
eyes for a few seconds.

Lawrence took Melody's arm and didn't say anything.
Suddenly it overwhelmed him, what Melody had been through

with her mom. He realized she had been very strong over the years. He had always looked at her bad behavior and assumed she was out of control, that she was bad. Now he felt a small understanding of what she experienced.

Comparing their situations helped him feel humble. They walked hand in hand back towards the hospital. When they came through the sliding doors, Auntie Red was sitting in the lobby. She had been crying.

"Lawrence, go up and say good-bye to your parents. We better head back."

Lawrence nodded and left.

# # #

Red and Melody sat looking at each other. "Auntie Red, I hope you still, that you still even like me," Melody's voice trailed off.

Auntie Red looked astonished. She paused, like she was gathering her thoughts. "Melody, I have always loved you, will always love you. It doesn't mean you were easy to live with. I am just happy everything seems so much better."

Melody nodded, not knowing how to reply. In a few minutes Lawrence returned looking subdued. During the ride home, each sat silently, absorbed in their own thoughts. A couple hours later, as they pulled into the dorm parking lot, Red started talking nervously.

"Um, Lawrence, we'll keep in touch. If, um, something should happen, we will get you home as soon as possible. Are you okay staying at school?"

"Yes," he replied numbly.

Red leaned over and squeezed Lawrence's arm and then Melody's knee.

"Okay, then hang in there," Red tried to smile.

Melody and Lawrence got out of the pickup. The afternoon was chilly and windy. Melody shivered and looked at Lawrence.

"Thanks for everything," He suddenly reached for her and hugged her so hard it pushed the breath out of her chest.

"Things will work out," she said when Lawrence finally released her.

Chapter Forty One

Holland remembered her feelings during Christmas break when she could tell something was happening at home. She felt she had been right on the money, smack dab on the money. It reminded her of watching a movie and dying to know the ending. But she just had to wait for the ending. No one could tell her how the movie ended. It would just have to be experienced.

One day, during the first week of March, Luke was not waiting for Holland after school. He still waited daily, even though it was cold and windy. She couldn't remember a day he didn't wait. Walking home with Luke was always one of the best parts of her day. He would tell her about his day, and ask questions about hers.

Some days Holland's mind was so preoccupied with all the goings-ons of her life, her distraction so intense, she felt sure talking to her seemed like talking to a wall. But Luke was not one to get angry, or feel put out. He was just one to accept her unconditionally, and she loved him for it.

Holland tried not to worry, but Luke not waiting for her raised a red flag. As soon as she walked in the house, Holland knew something had happened. It felt completely different.

Somehow she knew, without looking in their mother's bedroom, that she was gone. Her mother, who had not left the house since they moved in, who hardly even left her bedroom, was simply gone.

Holland knew her mother was gone, but the urgency she felt was to find Luke. "Luke!" She yelled, the sound sharply contrasting the quiet of the empty house.

Holland ran to his bedroom. Nothing. She ran to her mother's bedroom. The door was open. Her room was clean and there were two notes on the bed, one for Dad, one for her and no note for Luke.

Holland's heart thumped the insides of her chest, pounded at her lungs, made it difficult to breathe. She tore open her note.

"Dearest daughter Holland. I don't know quite how to say this, or even what to say. Clear to bottom of my heart, it aches. One of my biggest emotions is being so sorry. To say it is unfair to have a mother who has done what I have done is quite an understatement. To say I have not been doing well lately is an understatement. To try and express how much I love you, any words of my love for you are an understatement. The largest of all. I love you."

Holland, who had developed a cold, stone heart to-wards her mother, stifled a sob that, though very unwelcome, came up from somewhere shallow, not buried deeply at all. But Holland could not cry, would not cry until she knew where Luke was.

The letter continued, "Holland I guess if there is one thing I hope you can understand it is that none of this is your fault. I try telling myself that none of this is my fault either. But I can't say that with a clear conscience. I will always be your mother. I hope what I am doing will help me be able to be your mother, not just biologically, but really be your mom. You still have much living to do. I hope someday to attend your graduation from high school, and college, your wedding. Oh Holland, dear, you have so much ahead of you.

"I love your brilliant mind. I love your interest in words. I love your beautiful hair. I love your ability to somehow go on with a mother who has done what I have done. I love you from the depths of everything inside of me.

"I know you love Luke. I worry the most about him. He is too good and kind, and while that is wonderful, sometimes those are the people who take the worst beating from this Earth life experience. Help him.

"I plead with you to not give up on me. I am trying to do something. I am trying to get help so I can change all of this. I am trying something unconventional, since everything conventional gets me nowhere. I love you, my Holland girl. Don't give up on me. Mom."

Holland sat on the bed, filled up with emotions she thought she had put behind her, yet were right there, so nearby. Holland realized they had always been right there, right under the surface.

She stifled another sob and all the emotion that came with it. Not until she found Luke could she go there. She had a sick feeling about Luke. She tore open her dad's letter. She could not wait for him to read it to find out if it contained any clues as to where Luke went. That letter made her fight back emotion again, emotion for the hurt of it all. She realized acutely that their marriage may not make it, but no word about Luke.

Of course their mother would leave a note for him. But where was it? And where was Luke? She hoped her mother got help. She hoped her mother was all right, but her anxiety about Luke was foremost. It was all she could think of.

Holland's mind fought off panic. Luke wouldn't have gone home with a friend without telling her. Maybe he stayed after school. Holland hoped against hope, but it was all she had to go on.

She ran to Luke's school, ran to the door of his classroom. It was locked, so she pounded on the door. But the teacher was gone. She ran through the campus, to the front office door. The secretary was just getting ready to leave.

"I'm Holland, Luke Adams's sister. Have you seen Luke?" Holland tried not to sound desperate.

"Why, no. I haven't seen him. Is anything wrong?" The secretary looked concerned.

"No, no, well I don't think so. Luke just didn't come home after school." Holland felt breathless.

"Well be sure and let us know if he doesn't make it home," The secretary sounded worried.

"Okay." Holland was running back towards home. Half way home she turned and started running towards the dorm. By the time she made it there she was completely out of breath. She ran down the hall of the dorm to Lawrence's room. His door was open and he sat studying at his desk.

"Lawrence," was all she could say, trying to catch her breath.

"Holland! Are you all right?"

"Lawrence, I can't find Luke. And my mom left." Holland breathed out.

"What?" Lawrence looked confused.

Her voice filled with panic. She tried to slow down. "My mom left. Don't know where to. I can't find Luke."

"Where is your dad?" Lawrence's voice was beginning to register concern.

"I guess he is still at work."

"Did you call him?"

Holland realized she was doing everything out of order. She wasn't thinking clearly. "No, I went to Luke's school but they haven't seen him."

Lawrence was putting on his jacket. He took Holland by the arm. "Come on. Let's go back to your house. We'll call your dad and look around."

Once outside, she and Lawrence ran the entire way to her house. Inside, Holland led Lawrence to Luke's room. They looked around. Holland groaned when she saw it. It gave her a crushing fear. It was an envelope crumpled up by his bed. An envelope like the one her letter had been in. She unfolded it. It had Luke written on it, but Luke's letter wasn't there.

"Lawrence look!" Holland pulled her letter out of her back jean pocket. She left Luke a letter too, that means she didn't take him! So where is he?"

Lawrence looked at the two envelopes. "What did she say?" he asked.

Melody handed him her letter. He read it quickly, glancing at her a few times.

"And she left my dad one that I read." Holland pulled him to her mom's room.

Lawrence read that letter also. When he was finished he gasped a small sound and looked at Holland like he was an intruder.

Holland knew it was a lot of information to take in, but her panic about Luke overrode any emotion of embarrassment, even the embarrassment that Lawrence Yellowhair was now much more aware of the family dysfunction, the horrible, gaping mess.

"We should call your dad," he said levelly.

"No!" Holland yelled without thinking.

She sat on the edge of her mom's bed and put her head in her hands, ran her fingers through her blazing hair, tried to clear her mind to think about what was the best, quickest, way to find Luke.

"If I call him," she said, still panicky, but talking slower, "he'll tell me to wait here, until he can get here. I can't do that! I feel like things are really wrong, really bad. This is just not like Luke. I have to find him. I can't wait for my dad."

"You must tell him. You have to." Lawrence argued, urgency growing in his voice.

"I know. I know. But I can't wait here for him. I have to

look," she said in desperation.

"Okay, okay, so tell him and we will continue to look."

"Okay, yes, that is what I could do," Holland said, sorting her thoughts while she spoke. "Will you, will you help me?" She looked up at Lawrence, anguished.

"Of course!" he answered.

"We need a car," Holland said, trying to gather a plan. With that she ran to the garage. The family minivan was gone. "I can't believe it! She hasn't driven in years!" She ran back into the kitchen.

Just then the phone rang. Holland jumped a mile, and then grabbed the receiver. "Hello?" Relief soared through her as she heard Luke's voice, "Holland!" he whispered loudly.

"Luke where are you? Are you with Mom?" she demanded.

"I can't talk now Holland. I'm just calling to say I'm okay. I'm trying to help Mom. I'll call again when I can."

"What?" Holland yelled into the phone. "Where are you?"

"Reservation," Luke's voice said quietly before the phone went dead.

"Reservation? Why? Where on the reservation?" Holland yelled, knowing Luke was gone.

Holland looked at Lawrence in apprehensive agony.

"Look at the number! What number did he call from?"

Holland looked at the number. "I don't recognize it."

Lawrence nodded, "Okay, then we need to call your dad and the police."

Holland nodded, "Just promise me, we won't call until we are leaving for the reservation, so they don't stop me from looking. Can you get a car?"

"Cody can," he said. "I'll run back to the dorm and find Cody and we'll get a pickup. I will try to be back in ten minutes. Bring a warm jacket and maybe a little food. Promise me as soon as I leave, you will call your dad and the police!" Not waiting for her reply Lawrence ran out of the house.

Holland quickly decided to gather some things she would need first and then call. She grabbed some fruit out of the fridge, some granola bars, and a few bottles of water and stuffed them in a plastic grocery bag.

She grabbed a warm jacket and hastily put it on. She went to the phone and called her dad's cell phone. "Dad!" she said shakily when he answered.

"Holland? Is everything all right?"

"Dad, please listen to me, just listen. Mom is gone. She took the minivan. Luke is gone too. Somehow he is following her. I don't know where he is. A few minutes ago he called and said he was trying to help Mom. Said he was on the reservation. I don't know any more than that, but, I'm already looking for him!" Holland finished breathlessly.

"What?" he sounded dazed.

"Mom and Luke are gone! I'm looking for them, I'm leaving right now!"

"No, Holland, wait! Don't move an inch until I get there!" Dad was yelling.

Exactly what she knew he would say. "No! Dad, I can't wait. It might be too late! I'll call you. Dad, call the police, and Dad, I love you." Holland hung up the phone, relieved she had thought to tell her dad to call the police. She knew if she had a chance of getting out of town she had to hurry.

Holland wrote the number Luke called her from on a paper near the phone, then wrote it down again and shoved it in her jean's pocket. She ran back to her room and grabbed all the money she had out of her top drawer, not much, but at least enough for a tank of gas. She ran to the front porch, pleading in her mind for Lawrence to be there.

She paced the porch for a few minutes. She could hear the phone ringing. She ran back in and saw it was Dad's number. She wasn't answering that. She ran back outside, just as a pickup pulled up. Three people sat in the truck, Cody, Melody, and Lawrence. Holland wondered why in the world Melody was there but didn't have time to question, didn't have time to hear an explanation.

Chapter Forty Two

Holland ran to the passenger side. Lawrence jumped out and she scooted over next to Melody, then Lawrence crammed back in. The pickup cab was crowded with four.

Holland looked nervously over at Melody and Cody. "Hi," she said. "Thanks for helping me. We need to go to the reservation."

Cody pulled out and started down the road. "Hi, Holland," he said in his easygoing voice. "The reservation is awfully big. Do you know exactly where we need to go?"

Holland put her head back on the seat and closed her eyes, took a few deep breaths, and tried to gather her thoughts. "I don't know where. I don't have any idea. The only thing I know is Luke called me from a number. I have it here."

"Call the number," Cody said

"I have a cell phone," Melody said.

Holland mumbled, "Thanks," taking Melody's phone. Surprised she hadn't thought of calling it herself.

She dialed the number, the phone rang several times. An answering machine picked it up. It was her mom's voice. Holland had forgotten her mom even had a phone. She wondered how Luke had it.

She hung up, not leaving a message. "It's my mom's cell phone."

"You didn't even know it was your mom's number?" Melody asked, disgust tingeing her surprise.

"I . . . I . . . she never uses it. I forgot she even had one," she said miserably.

Holland saw Lawrence give Melody a look. Then he said, "Holland, we need to tell them what's going on." Holland cringed, wondering again why Melody was even there. Lawrence seemed to read her mind, "When I was running back to the dorm, they drove by. It was a lucky break."

Then, not waiting for Holland to reply, he went on. "Melody and Cody, some hard things are going on in Holland's

family right now. Her mom left today. Her little brother is somehow following her, or something. Holland is trying to find him.
You don't have to come, but we could use your help."

Holland saw Melody's eyes widen in surprise. Melody
looked at her, staring intently.

Cody said, "I'm in. We'll find him."

Holland breathed out a sigh, "Oh thank you, thank you
Cody."

"Me too," Melody said quietly.

"Thanks, Melody," Holland replied nervously.

"Where do we even start?" Holland asked. And then
before anyone could answer she added, "Is there like a main
road that runs from here through the reservation?"

"Yes. Now you're thinking, Holland," Lawrence nodded,
sounding old. "There is a main road from here to Chinle. Your
mom would at least have to start on that road."

"Okay!" Holland said, feeling a little hopeful. "Maybe I
could try texting the number. Maybe Luke can text, but not talk
right now."

Melody handed her phone back. She quickly texted
asking, "Luke, this is Holland, can you text me?"

In a few seconds, a message came back. "Yes."

"Where are you? How come you can text but not talk? How did you get mom's phone? Are you okay?"

"I can't tell you everything. I'm hiding in the back of the minivan under a blanket. Mom doesn't know I'm here. I grabbed Mom's phone before I left. I talked when Mom left the car for a few minutes."

"Where are you? Tell Mom you are there! Tell her to take you home! How did you know about Mom's phone?"

"I saw the phone when I helped her clean her room at Thanksgiving. I don't know where I am. I can't see. I'm not leaving Mom. She needs my help. She is not herself and you know it."

"How do you know you are on the reservation?"

"Because she is talking a lot out loud, like you do. She talked about going to a medicine man on the reservation for help. Holland, I'm afraid of skinwalkers."

Even though Holland knew he didn't know, she desperately texted again. "Where are you going? Everyone will be looking for you. They will know the license plate. How did you know she was leaving and how did you get in the back of the minivan?"

There was never another text. Holland felt her panic level rise again. She kept checking Melody's phone. She felt sick to her stomach. She wanted to cry, but was not about to do that in front of everyone.

"I don't know what to do. I can't leave him with my mom. I don't know what . . . what she will do. She is not herself," Holland said, her voice shaking.

"Maybe you should call your dad. See what is happening on his end," Melody said. Holland noticed she actually sounded sincere.

"Okay, that's a good idea. He will just tell me to get home. But I won't. I won't leave Luke out there. I have to find him," Holland was adamant.

"Are you afraid your mom will hurt him?" Cody broke his silence.

"No, yes . . . no. She would never hurt him on purpose. But lately, she scares me. Luke thinks he has to take care of everyone. He told me he is afraid of skinwalkers. Skinwalkers! It doesn't make sense, being afraid of something make believe when he should be afraid of our mother."

The truck cab went silent. Holland looked at Lawrence, Melody, and Cody. One look let her know they didn't think skinwalkers were some made up fantasy. One look let her see that they believed in them.

"Really?" Holland said unbelieving. "You guys really believe in skinwalkers?"

"Holland, don't talk lightly about what you don't understand," Lawrence said kindly but seriously.

Lawrence's comment completely stunned Holland. She felt thoroughly the outcast of the cab. But she couldn't worry about that. With hands still shaking she dialed her dad's number.

"Dad," she said when he answered.

"Holland, where are you? Come home right now. I don't need to have you lost too!"

"I won't come home until I find Luke. He's in the back of the minivan under a blanket, trying to help Mom. Have you heard anything?"

"What? Luke is with Mom, but she doesn't know it?" Dad's voice betrayed his worry. "The local police and reservation police are looking for the van right now. I want you to come home now." That time he was firm.

She ignored his command, "Dad, do you know any medicine men she would go to? Did she talk to you about her plans?"

It was his turn to ignore her. "Holland who are you with? What can you hope to achieve?" He tried pleading, "Come home."

Holland looked at Lawrence, then Melody and Cody. She knew if she told her Dad whose truck she was in, they would immediately have the license number. She breathed deeply. "Call this number if you have any news Dad. Don't call if you don't have any. I want to save the battery in case Luke gets a hold of me."

"Holland, Holland! Don't you dare!" Dad barked.

She disconnected the call. She looked at Lawrence and tried to smile bravely, instead of bursting into tears. In the late afternoon sun she noticed his eyes were not completely black, but a dark, dark brown. They were beautiful, but she pulled herself away.

Holland wondered what she could accomplish, if they found Luke, or if it all was just a mad chase, because as soon as their mother knew Luke was there, surely she would turn around and bring him home.

She had to pull her thoughts together, do her best thinking, be smart about her approach. She remembered Luke saying their mother talked to herself. She marveled how strange it had to be for her, being out of the house after so many months, and driving!

Holland wondered what state her mom was in, hopefully more like the state at Christmas, than Thanksgiving. She searched her mind for anything that could help. She remembered a clue.

"Do Navajo medicine men perform ceremonies on white people?" she asked quietly, as Cody turned off the interstate and headed the same way the bus had gone when she went with Lawrence to his home.

Lawrence answered, "Yes, there are some medicine men that will. It's controversial, but yes."

"Why would it be controversial?"

"Because some ceremonies are meant to help and cleanse a person from white man's evil influences," Melody said, seeming happy to give Holland the information.

"Medicine men are mostly very good, very upright men, who want the best for the Navajo," Lawrence said in his old voice.

Cody broke in. "Holland some medicine men have actually murdered a close family member or someone they should be close to, as part of an initiation to become a medicine man." Cody glanced at her and continued quietly. "A few medicine men are seeking the wrong kind of power."

She blinked a few times, but could not blink away the man from the train wreck watching her. "Luke said she was going to one," she moaned. Then her mind started working again. Her mother would have had to make calls, or looked on the internet, or both. Luke needed to check the cell phone. Her dad needed to check the internet history, and phone records.

Holland first texted Luke. "If you can, check for phone numbers recently called. See if there are several to same number."

Holland dialed her dad again. "Dad," she talked quickly, trying to avoid his lecture. "Check the phone records. Mom had to call, or somehow find a medicine man. Check the internet history too. They might give us a clue."

"Holland, the police are already tracing the phone and the location of the phone you are on," he said wearily.

"Good. Still check the records, call every number if you have to." Holland hung up again.

"I know one," Melody said softly. "I know a medicine man that does ceremonies on whites."

Chapter Forty Three

"There's a medicine man, who would do a ceremony on a white person, at Cornfields, a place called Cornfields," Melody looked at Lawrence, he nodded, agreeing.

"How close is it?" Holland asked.

"About thirty miles," Cody answered.

It's a complete shot in the dark." Lawrence shook his head. "But Melody and I have been to this medicine man's hogan before. . ."

Holland faced Lawrence. "It's worth a try. She could be right. I know things about her. She might know things about me."

"What? What are you talking about?" Melody asked, her old disgust towards Holland returning. "How would you know anything about me? Unless. . ." Melody looked at Lawrence with fire in her eyes.

"I didn't tell her anything," Lawrence said, looking squarely at Melody. "She knows though."

"Knows! How could she know anything unless someone told her?" Melody's voice was rising.

"I had, I had a dream about you, all right?" Holland yelled back.

"What a liar!" Melody fumed. "You had a dream about me? Yeah right!"

"I had a dream. I saw you and your mom when you were little. I know about her drinking. I know about you and Lawrence. I saw it all. I know Melody. I know about your mom." She went from yelling, to talking in a weary whisper.

"You know about my mom?" Melody sat in subdued confusion. She looked at Lawrence coldly. "Does she know about your mom, about last week?"

Lawrence stuttered. "No, I, I haven't told her. I haven't had a chance."

"What about your mother?" Holland looked at Lawrence, alarmed. "Is she okay?"

"Well my mom is a waitress at Denny's. She makes minimum wage and all the tips she can carry in her pocket." Cody said dryly. "Does anyone want to know about her?"

Everyone sat in frozen silence. Holland could not help herself, she started laughing, and half crying, and then in spite of the situation, all her emotion came up and out in the laugh. Nervously watching her, Lawrence joined in, and even though Melody fought it off, she could not help herself. Cody sat with a big grin, very pleased with himself.

When she could finally compose herself Holland said, "Lawrence, really, is your mother okay."

Melody interrupted, "We went to Flagstaff to see her last week."

Holland looked at Melody, then turned to Lawrence, trying to hide her hurt. "Is she okay?" she asked again very quietly.

Lawrence grimaced at Melody and then turned to Holland. "No, Holland, she had a very rough go of it for a few days last week. My dad says she's doing a little better, but she is still in the hospital."

Cody once again came through. "Holland, don't feel

bad. I will take you to Denny's to see my mom."

Everyone smiled again. But Holland felt stung knowing Lawrence went to Melody for comfort, then took Melody to Flagstaff when he needed more comfort.

But none of that could matter. She had to find Luke.

They sat in silence for several miles. "What if I'm wrong?" Melody asked. "What if your mom is not in Cornfields?" Then before anyone could answer, she astonished everyone. "Holland, I'm sorry I told you about going to Flagstaff with Lawrence. It was small of me."

Holland thought about the times she knew she made Melody jealous and did not care a wit. Holland pushed a smile into her lips at Melody, appreciative of her humility. "If my mother isn't in Cornfields, I guess . . . I guess we should go back. I don't know."

Then, completely overwhelmed at the thought of not finding Luke, of him being alone and scared on the reservation, and thinking he had to save their mother; it was all more than she could handle. She started crying. She had held it in since reading her mother's letter. The harder Holland tried to stop, the more it came. She felt like a blubbering idiot. Lawrence put his arm around her and pulled her close.

But Holland remembered the sting she had just felt and did not want to give it back to Melody. She tried to stiffen, to pull away, but she could not stop crying. She cried over Luke, over her mother, over Lawrence and Melody.

She regained her composure enough to say, "Cody, I could really use something funny right now."

Cody did not miss a beat. "Sometimes life makes us laugh, sometimes it makes us cry. You white girls sure do both well." But then as if to comfort her he added, "But that's okay; I'd be crying too if my brother was missing."

Holland smiled at him, glad the sun was just going down, maybe the redness of her face wasn't showing as much. Lawrence kept his arm around her. In spite of knowing about taking Melody to Flagstaff, she wanted to snuggle into him and yet she didn't want to in front of Melody.

As the darkness worked to overtake the day, Holland felt weak, all her emotion drained. Her head hurt. She said a silent prayer for Luke, and for her mother. Suddenly, out the side of her eye, she saw something and did a double take.

It was almost dark, but she could barely see an animal

running alongside the pickup, keeping up with the truck. She looked again. It was not an animal, but it was. It was running on two legs and as tall as a man, yet looked like a wolf.

She practically jumped onto Lawrence's lap. "Lawrence!" She screamed. "Something is running next to us!"

She saw Melody put her head down and Cody take one hand and hold it to his face, like someone trying to shade his face from the sun.

Lawrence grabbed her face, pulled her to look at him. "Holland, listen to me. Don't look at it!"

Holland looked at him, unable to focus, "What, what is it?"

Lawrence responded more firmly, "Don't look at it! Since we have spoken of *them* we are more at risk to see one."

"What? What are you talking about?" Holland stiffened.

Lawrence continued, "I hoped this would not happen."

"You've got to get her to not watch it!" Cody spoke loudly.

"Put your head down!" Melody yelled.

Holland felt a chill down her back. "You've got to be kidding. Is this just all to try and scare me?" She yelled to everyone in the pickup.

"Holland, how could this be us playing a trick on you. This is real," Lawrence said in astonishment at her question.

Cody was driving much faster. But the thing only ran faster too, keeping up. She could not stop glancing at it.

"Holland! You've got to quit watching it," Lawrence said urgently.

"How? I can't stop!"

Lawrence again took hold of her face. He pulled it close to his. She could feel his warm breath on her skin. "Look at me, take a breath."

Holland focused on his eyes, even with the approaching darkness she could see them. She breathed in deeply.

"That's right, keep looking at me. Another deep breath."

She could feel the pickup go even faster, skidding towards the night. She glanced again, the thing was lagging behind.

"Don't Holland. Look at me, only at me."

She looked again at Lawrence. His eyes looked black again.

"Skinwalkers? Just what are they? How could something run as fast as a truck?" Holland asked incredulously.

"I can't speak of it. Now is not the time. Just don't underestimate this," Lawrence answered.

Holland sat dumbfounded, scared and astonished that she felt fear at something so outrageous. She could not believe that she had actually seen something which five minutes earlier she would have sworn on her life was only some superstition.

Cody interrupted her thoughts. "We'll be there pretty quick. Maybe we should make a plan."

Holland peered out the window into the darkness. She could not see the thing. Lawrence pulled her face to his again. "Don't," he firmly stated again.

"So why did you two come to this medicine man before?" Cody asked, nodding toward Lawrence and Melody.

"Not now, Cody. Now's not the time," Melody shuddered.

"Then, just tell me how to get there," Cody said, sounding less laid-back.

As they neared the tiny town, a few lights fought through the darkness. Holland could not shake the overpowering fear, and foreboding that she felt. She worried sick about

Luke.

"Will that thing find us?" Holland asked."

"Hopefully we ditched it," Cody looked around.

"Turn here," Melody motioned to Cody.

They pulled onto an isolated dirt road. They drove over a cattle guard, seeing a small light and the outline of a hogan ahead.

"That's it," Melody said, not hiding the fear in her voice.

"My mother's van!" Holland heart leaped in her throat.

Cody killed the pickup lights.

"Maybe we should park here and walk." Lawrence said cautiously. "If Holland's mom is not here, we can leave quickly, and not cause a commotion."

They got out, and Holland started to run. "She's here, of course she is here. She has to be in the hogan, maybe Luke is still in the minivan. I can get him, and we can go. No, I should get my mother . . ." Holland wondered what she wanted.

Cody caught her first pulling her back. "Wait Holland. We can't just charge in. Let's decide what we are going to do."

"We're going to get my brother!" Holland tried to be quiet, but cringed at the loudness of her voice in the night.

"But what if he's not still here? Do you want your mother to know you're here?" Lawrence asked.

"I don't care if she knows either way. I just have to find Luke!" Holland pleaded.

Melody pulled Holland back several yards. "Holland, I know this medicine man is evil. That's why we need to be careful."

"How do you know?" Holland said fighting frustration. "How would you know?"

"For one, he does ceremonies on whites." Melody reminded her. "Sometimes people, Navajos and whites, want a ceremony when they really shouldn't be having one, when it's inappropriate. A good medicine man would say no."

"If he is dangerous, what would he be doing to my mom?" Holland felt a new wave of fear.

"Well he could be involving powers for help that shouldn't be used, powers meant for evil," Lawrence replied.

Holland's head swirled. She felt engulfed in a science-fiction movie. She thought of the thing she had just seen running alongside the pickup. She knew Lawrence had always believed in his Navajo traditions. Traditions, Holland realized she did not begin to understand. There was so much she didn't know about him.

She thought about the ceremony for Lawrence's mother. It had felt strange and different, but none of it struck her as voodoo. The ceremony just seemed another culture's way. She knew all cultures had good, and evil. Another chill seized her back.

"I have to get Luke," she said, her voice shaking, desperate. "I'll be quiet. I just want to knock on the van window to see if he's in there." She started toward the van again.

Everyone followed. She knocked softly on the window. She knocked several times. No Luke. Holland's heart sank. She wanted to go up to the hogan, and see if her mother and Luke were inside.

Lawrence took her arm, providing much needed support.

"I'm going to the hogan," she proclaimed fiercely.

"I'll back the pickup up close, but we need to get out of here." Cody said, obviously worried.

Walking to the door of the hogan, with Lawrence a few steps back, she felt something rush around her, quickly circling her several times. It felt like a cold, unearthly wind.

But whatever it was, it certainly was not wind, because she felt it, felt the evilness of it. She felt it look at her and breathe on her. She fell to her knees in fear. Lawrence came to her side.

"Did you, did you feel that?" Holland could barely speak.

"Yes, Holland, whatever you do, don't look at it if it comes back. We have to go!" Lawrence whispered, pulling her back. "It's another skinwalker; this one is faster, more dangerous."

Melody, who was a few steps back, did not whisper, but spoke loudly. "We have to go now!"

"No! Not without Luke!" Holland's concern for Luke became greater than her fear.

"Holland we are not safe here!" His whisper grew more urgent.

"Go back then, but I'm not!"

She felt the evil being whirl back and run around her and Lawrence, so quickly she couldn't have looked even if she was brave enough to try. Again she felt the evil suck energy out of her.

Holland stumbled to her feet, unaware if Lawrence followed. She staggered to the door and pounded. Everything went silent. The evilness whirled around her again, its breath on her neck.

Holland pounded on the door again, trying to yell, "Luke, Mom! Luke, Mom! Please!"

No answer came. The skinwalker circled her again, closer, so close she felt the form of it rubbing against her. Holland's head reeled and she struggled to keep her feet.

Lawrence grabbed her, pulling her away from the hogan, pulling her to the pickup. Holland fought him, crying, yelling, and telling him she would not leave Luke. She hit him and tried to scratch his face. But Lawrence held strong, stronger than she thought him capable. He pinned her arms to her sides and lifted her, running the best he could towards the truck.

Holland screamed, yelling, "No, no, no, please no!"

When Lawrence made it to the pickup, Melody and Cody were already in. Cody had the pickup started. As Lawrence opened the door, the dome light let out an eerie glow, like no amount of light could overcome the darkness, the evil. Holland glanced around, looking for the thing in the darkness.

Lawrence shoved Holland into the cab and pushed in behind her, slamming the door. "Drive!" He yelled at Cody.

Cody turned on the headlights and peeled out in a lurch and cloud of dust.

"No, no, no," Holland kept repeating. "Please, please, let me get Luke!" She tried to climb over Lawrence to the door handle.

Lawrence wrapped his arms around Holland, holding her down, "Holland, Holland, Holland, we had to leave."

As the pickup sped away, Holland was beside herself. She couldn't believe they forced her to leave Luke and her mother. She couldn't believe they didn't care anymore than that.

She flung Lawrence's arms off her, hating him, hating them all. Suddenly in the headlights, crouched next to the road, sat Luke.

"Luke!" Holland screamed. "Stop, stop the truck!"

Cody slammed on the brakes. The cloud of dust following the truck engulfed them, making it impossible to see. Holland opened the door. "Luke!" she screamed again. "Luke, Luke!"

But Luke did not answer, at least she could not hear him. Holland scrambled to where she had seen Luke, reaching for him, yelling his name. She ran straight into him, knocking them off their feet. They both lay in the dirt, choking.

"Luke?" Holland said again.

"Holland? Holland is that you?" Luke stammered in disbelief.

He plunged his arms around her. She saw Lawrence kneeling beside them.

Holland sat up, still sputtering with the dust that filled her mouth. "Luke, are you okay? Are you okay? Where is our mother?"

Darkness and dust prevented Holland from seeing his face, but she could hear the fear in his voice. "Holland, she's back at the hogan! We have to go back!"

"Holland we have to get out of here," Lawrence pulled at her.

"Are you sure she's there?" Holland ignored Lawrence.

"I just pounded on the door and nobody answered."

"She's there!" Luke's voice grew more shrill. "And, could you feel what else is there?"

Lawrence was pulling on Holland and Luke to get back in the pickup.

"I'm going back," she shouted. "I'm going back for my mother, even if I have to walk."

"We can't Holland," Lawrence said in a determined voice. "It's too dangerous. You don't know what you are facing."

"I don't care!" Holland yelled as loud as she could. "My mother needs me. I can't leave!"

"At least get in the truck," he pleaded.

Holland saw that Melody and Cody were out of the pickup, standing behind Lawrence.

"No!" You will drive off. Then turning to Luke she said, "Luke you should go with them!"

"No!" Luke was as determined as her.

Lawrence shook his head, then said desperately, "Okay, okay! I'll go back with you. But I promise you Holland Adams, it will not be good!"

Lawrence repeated it to Melody and Cody, "I am going

back with Holland and Luke."

"What?" Melody and Cody chorused in disbelief.

"Lawrence, please don't go." Melody begged.

"I'm going," Lawrence was resolute. "I would go back too, if it were my mother and so would you two."

"Get in! You dumb assholes! I'll take you," Cody barked.

They squeezed in. Cody wheeled the truck around and headed back for the hogan. "Don't expect me to sing at your funeral. We'll all be killed."

Holland turned to Lawrence. "I know you don't want to speak of them, but you've got to help me understand. What is a skinwalker?"

Lawrence swallowed hard. He put his arm around her neck and pulled her in close to his mouth. "It's one of us Holland. It's a Navajo."

"A Navajo?" The force of it hit her.

"It's a Navajo. One who desires evil," Lawrence was so near.

"Why would someone desire evil? I don't get it," she tasted the dust on her lip.

"There is nothing to get," was all he said.

And then he spoke to everyone in the cab. "I wouldn't be surprised if your mother has a hex on her and that is why she wouldn't answer. We need to get her out and put her in the back of the pick-up. Then hold her down until we get her to come to her senses," Lawrence said, sorting it out.

"How do we accomplish that?" Holland spoke with fear.

Lawrence shivered, "I don't know. It's the skinwalker we will have to distract,"

Holland's heart pounded between her ears and Luke, practically sitting on her, shook uncontrollably.

"I think I know what the skinwalker is doing." Luke spoke with a shaky voice. "I think the skinwalker protects the hogan. When I tried to sneak up to the hogan to get Mom, it grabbed me."

"It grabbed you?" Holland felt horror.

"It picked me up and ran from the house and threw me. That's how I ended up near the road," Luke said, like he couldn't quite believe it.

He spoke again, as if to himself. "I couldn't believe it, that thing carried me and ran, but it felt as smooth as being in a car."

She had a hard time comprehending. "Are you hurt?"

"I think I landed okay. It was so strong."

"If your intentions are not evil, a skinwalker has less power over you," Cody said solemnly. "I'm sure it wanted to harm you, but could not."

The pickup neared the cattle guard again. In the hogan, a small light continued to glow from the window.

Cody and Lawrence both started talking. "We need to get in the hogan. We'll probably have to carry her out," Cody said.

"Somehow we need to distract the skinwalker," Lawrence said.

Melody who had been quiet spoke, not hiding her fear. "I think I know how. I think if we could get the medicine man out of the hogan, somehow pull him away, I think the skinwalker will follow the medicine man. He is protecting him, not the hogan. Then you guys could get in the hogan and carry her to the truck."

"Could it work?" Holland asked petrified. "How do we get the medicine man to come out?"

"Break the hogan window," Lawrence said. "You girls find a big rock and toss it right through the window. Luke you need to stay in the back of the truck, as soon as we get your mother here, you need to start talking to her, bringing her to."

"I'm afraid of that thing, but I'll do anything," Luke replied resolutely.

"Hopefully with all the distractions, it won't notice you," Cody sounded unsure. "The only hope we have is to move really fast and be out of here before they can make decisions."

Holland heard Luke swallow a lump in his throat. She felt sick with fear. But they had to go on. Cody pulled the truck to a stop, but kept the headlights on. Holland spotted a few large rocks next to the fence and cattle guard. She hoped Melody saw them too.

Quickly, they got out. Luke scrambled into the bed of the pickup. Everyone else started running. Holland's fear made her legs feel heavy and slow.

Cody and Lawrence headed towards the side of the east-facing door of the hogan. Holland picked up the largest rock she could carry. She saw Melody grab one also. Holland and Melody ran straight to the hogan.

In the split second before Holland threw her rock through the window, she saw her mother, lying on a table in the hogan. The medicine man stood over her, with a pair of scissors. He held a large chunk of her mother's strawberry red hair in his hand.

The rocks went through the window on the south side. With an earth-shattering sound the rocks broke the window, glass flying.

The skinwalker immediately circled the girls and the door of the hogan cracked open. Holland felt everyone freeze, not sure how to proceed. She was stunned when Melody cried out, not to the skinwalker but to the medicine man. "I know you. I know what you do."

The evil thing reached out, trying to grab for Melody. Holland immediately wrapped her arms around Melody, yelling, "Leave her alone!"

Melody screamed louder, "I know you. I know what you do. Give us the woman."

The hogan door opened fully. Holland gasped. It was the man from the train wreck. The tall skinny man stood dressed in jeans and a tee-shirt, his long hair braided down his back, smiling the same smile that Holland had seen in her mind. The thing was immediately at his side.

"Who are you?" The medicine man called, peering towards the girls. "What do you want?"

"We want Holland's mom." Melody said loudly.

The medicine man snorted. "Who are you to tell me what to do?" His voice rising as he walked toward them. "Who are you to think you can threaten me?" The evil thing seemed to dance and whirl eagerly around the medicine man as he approached Holland and Melody.

Again Holland felt like her knees would buckle and she would fall to her knees. She hoped Cody and Lawrence were getting her mother. She wondered if they could get her in the pickup and how she and Melody could make a break from the medicine man.

She caught her breath, when again, Melody spoke loudly, repeating the same thing. "I know who you are, and what you are doing. I know what you did to my mom. You did not help her."

Holland understood how Melody knew him. She wondered if Melody's words would make things worse. As the medicine man neared them, the skinwalker started swirling around them. Again, Holland felt the energy drain out of her. A feeling of cold, dead space seemed to push in, squeeze, then suffocate her.

The medicine man waved his arm and hissed a Navajo word that Holland did not know.

Holland breathed deeply, but could not catch her breath, "I know you, from the train wreck."

"Yes I saw you. I saw when you saw me. I've seen the times you've seen me in your mind."

"What? How?" Holland felt the terror waving up in her chest would surely cause her to pass out, but she remained standing.

"Holland loves her mom," Melody spoke forcefully. "She is only here because she loves her mom. You cannot stop her from loving her mom, wanting to help her. You know the help you claim to give will not really help her."

The medicine man stopped short a few feet away, when Melody spoke of love. Holland saw his face contort into an ugly grimace. "I know what she feels for her mother. I know when she sees me in her mind," he growled.

Holland stepped towards the medicine man, in front of Melody. "I do love my mother. You can't stop us from taking her." The thing circled her, grabbing at her. Holland felt faint. The medicine man took in a deep breath and said nothing. Melody grabbed Holland's arm and started running.

When they got to the pickup, Holland saw Lawrence and Cody in the back with Luke and her mother.

"Mother. You got my mother," Holland cried, climbing into the bed. She crawled to her mother, but she seemed in a deep sleep, her head on Luke's lap.

Holland glanced towards the hogan, but the medicine man just stood watching. She could no longer feel the skin-walker whirling around her.

Cody jumped over the side and into the cab, peeling out in a cloud of dust. Everyone held on.

They drove back to the highway. Cody squealed onto the pavement and drove for a mile, then pulled over. Holland locked eyes with Lawrence. She couldn't believe what had just happened. It felt beyond comprehension.

"My home is closer than Holbrook," Lawrence said. "We'll go there for the night. We need to call your father."

He gave Cody instructions to his home. Cody climbed back in the truck. Holland finally noticed it was freezing in the back.

After a few minutes the cold woke her mom. She sat straight up in confusion, and did not speak. Luke wrapped his arms around her.

Holland sat feeling dazed, despite the frigid air whistling in their faces. She could not sort through the events, make sense of any of it. It all seemed like a bad dream. It couldn't possibly have been real.

She watched Melody, who watched Luke and her mother. Lawrence stared out the side. She shivered wondering if he was watching for skinwalkers.

It seemed like just a few minutes, but it had to have been many, when they pulled off the highway onto the dirt road that led to Lawrence's home. They pulled up to the front porch.

"My dad will be Flagstaff with my mother." Lawrence said softly.

"I'll go to Auntie Red's. Cody, come with me," Melody said, climbing out of the truck.

"They will call my father and he'll be here by morning.

That is probably what needs to happen." Lawrence said, sounding tired.

Lawrence offered his hand and helped her mother out of the truck. Holland didn't wonder at her mother's quietness. It was all new territory. Luke and Holland each took one of her arms and walked her slowly to the porch.

Chapter Forty Four

The rest of the night was a blur to Holland. Her mother was awake, but clearly confused. Holland helped her wash up, and saw the big chunk of her hair missing. She put her in Lawrence's fresh-smelling bed. Holland sat on the edge of the bed, with so many questions. But her mother was asleep in two minutes.

Holland called her dad, told him they had found Luke and Mom, that both were safe.

"I'm coming to get you," her dad sounded angry and relieved at the same time.

"You will never find this place, Dad." Holland said wearily. "We will come home first thing in the morning." And not waiting for his reply she added, "Tell the police."

Holland took a quick shower and put on some sweats of Antonia's that Lawrence loaned her. She crawled into a sleeping bag in the living room next to Luke, assuming Lawrence was in his parent's room.

She whispered. "Luke, are you okay?"

"Holland, you came. I don't know what would have happened if you hadn't."

She smiled. "Of course I came. But I can't believe it all. It doesn't feel real."

"The man that ran into the train, he went to the same medicine man. It's real Holland. It's real." Luke said, and fell asleep.

Holland could not sleep. She replayed the events over and over. She wondered how Luke knew the man at the train wreck went to the same medicine man. She wondered a million things.

After a while, Lawrence came in from his parent's room. He got a pillow off the couch and lay by Holland on the floor. Her heart pounded. It surprised her that her heart still had the energy to pound.

"Holland," he said quietly. "Are you all right?"

"Yes," she said, rolling on her side towards Lawrence, the hall light giving just enough light to see his beautiful face.

"You are incredibly brave," he whispered.

"I was incredibly scared," she said feeling sleepy.

Lawrence smiled and kissed her, a long, incredibly nice kiss.

Holland fell asleep.

Chapter Forty Five

Early the next morning, when Holland woke, Luke was still sound asleep. From the sounds of it, everyone in the house was still sleeping.

Holland crawled out of the sleeping bag and put on her shoes. She wanted to walk down to the wash, before Lawrence knew and could stop her.

Sneaking out of the house, the early morning sunshine was fighting to warm the cold of the night. The freshness of the day made last night feel even more impossible.

The wash was a deep one. A few huge cottonwoods lined its sides and on the sandy floor lay a few giant old logs. The wash walls jutted in and out of the dirt.

Holland found a trail to get to the bottom. The sun

warmed her face and the world felt normal. She sat on a huge log, closed her eyes, enjoying the comfort of the sun.

"Hi," said Melody sitting next to her.

Holland jumped. "H . . . hi," she stammered.

"Do you want to walk down the wash a bit?" Melody said.

Holland took off her shoes to walk in the warm sand. They walked quietly, farther down the wash. "So your mom went to that medicine man too?" Holland finally asked.

"Yes, when she fell off the wagon."

"I know your mom didn't raise you for a lot of years." Strangely Holland didn't feel nervous to be having this conversation.

Melody replied, "I didn't know your mom was having such a hard go of it."

"Your mom is doing better now?" Holland asked.

"Well things aren't perfect, but yes she is doing better." Melody stopped, and hesitantly added, "Your mom could pull it together."

"Can you discuss the skinwalker?" Holland asked tentatively. "I mean, I didn't even know about those things, I didn't even know they existed."

"We, we don't like to discuss skinwalkers. Just doing so, opens up the opportunity to encounter one."

Holland shivered. "I know they are real. I do know that now. Luke said the man who drove his pickup into the train had been to the same medicine man. Have you heard that?"

Melody's eyes shot over in surprise. "No. I hadn't heard that, but if it's true . . . well it means a lot of things."

They stopped walking. Each lost in their own thoughts. "About Lawrence." Holland said.

"Shh." Melody stopped her, smiling. "I won't bury my weapons of war when it comes to him."

Holland grinned, "I agree. But, I'm jealous of your whole history with him. He has always loved you."

"What's not to love . . ." Melody smiled back. "But since we are being honest, I'm jealous of how you two light up like Christmas trees whenever you're together."

Holland nodded, the thought making her happy. She touched Melody's arm. "I wouldn't believe anything about last night if I hadn't experienced it."

"I suppose none of us would believe anything much

about life, unless we experienced it," Melody answered. "And Holland, don't be too hard on your mom. That man, that medicine man, he makes big promises, when someone is in a low spot. My mom fell for it too. He didn't try to help her stop drinking; he tried to use her for his power and gain."

Holland gulped. "How could your mom, or mine, give him power."

"It's complicated; there is a lot to it. Did you notice he cut some of your mom's hair?"

"Yes, he took a big hunk of it."

"He will use the hair, the hair of a white woman, for ceremonies in the future. Anytime a medicine man uses a ceremony for personal gain, it is not a ceremony that will help, or heal anything."

Holland realized once again that she was barely scratching the surface of understanding the Navajo culture. There was so much to it; it would take a life time to understand. Then she thought of her mother, who understood probably less than she did. Her mother had become discouraged that nothing she tried for her depression worked and decided to try something unconventional. Holland could not blame her. "I guess I should look at it like at least she tried something," she replied.

Melody nodded. The wash wound around to a place where huge cottonwoods bordered along the top, their roots partly exposed down the sides of the wash. The roots were nearly as large as the trees.

Melody ran her hands along one of the exposed roots, made smooth from years of weather. "In my culture, our roots arc important. Can I ask you a question?"

Holland shrugged her shoulders, "Sure."

"Does your mom love you?"

"What? What do you mean?" Holland felt annoyed and confused.

"Does your mom love you?" Melody persisted.

"Yeah, I guess so. I don't know. Yeah I think she does," Holland said wrinkling her nose, wondering.

Melody added. "I mean our moms have so many problems, so do you think your mom still loves you?"

Holland felt emotion welling up inside of her, hot and eager to escape. "My mother hasn't really been able to, um, be a mother for a while, a long while. I think it hurts her even more than it hurts me, because she does love me. As bad as I've reacted to it all, she really still loves me."

"I know my mom loves me too," Melody said quietly. "My mom has been far from a perfect mom, the kind of mom she wishes she were. I guess even if you're not perfect you can still love your kids."

The truthfulness of what Melody said was ringing in Holland's head. She had not thought of it, had absolutely never thought of it.

Melody smiled at Holland and said. "I bet you never dreamed this conversation would happen."

"Do you believe in dreams?" Holland asked, wanting to share her part of the story. "Because I've had two about you. I've seen things about you and I don't really understand why. I mean I've even wondered if I'm having dreams, shouldn't I have them about how to help my mother or something?"

Melody looked thoughtful, and continued to run her hand along one of the smooth exposed roots. "The Navajo say dreams that mean anything only happen for special reasons, extraordinary reasons. I don't understand why you had dreams about my life. But I believe you did."

Holland caught her breath, "I dreamed about this. Right

here in this wash. I saw us talking as friends."

Melody looked Holland in the eyes, "Then what is happening must have meaning."

"I wish we could walk out of this wash and everything would just be fixed." Holland said sighing.

"If everything was fixed, we wouldn't find out the meaning." Melody replied.

Holland looked at Melody, her new friend, and felt happy, incredibly happy.

Jill Lewis spent her childhood in Snowflake, Arizona. The town was close to the Navajo reservation, and Lewis went to Snowflake High School, which had a Native American dormitory.

Lewis received her master's degree in therapeutic counseling from Northern Arizona University. She lives in Snowflake and works for the Snowflake School District. She spent three years working at Holbrook High school, the same school her protagonists attend in her new young adult novel.

Lewis has always been interested in Navajo culture. She enjoys collecting Native American jewelry and learning the history behind each piece.

Lewis has been married for forty-one years. She has five children and seventeen grandchildren, with one more on the way!